MARTYR

STERLING FALLS ROGUES
BOOK 3

S. MASSERY

INTRODUCTION

Hello dear reader!

Martyr is the third and final book in the Sterling Falls Rogues series. It is necessary to have read the first two books, *Nemesis* and *Warrior*, prior to this.

Artemis's story deals with some very difficult subject matter, including drug abuse, sex trafficking, rape, suicidal thoughts, and self harm.

If you'd like to know a bit more about some side characters and Artemis's history, dive into the short prequel story, Terror (available here: https://BookHip. com/HMPRACQ).

Happy reading!

xoxo,
Sara

PART 1

LYSSA

MY LIFE IS a series of flashes.

Memories. Sounds. Emotions.

The memories sting. Years of being rubbed on sandpaper should've smoothed my edges. It should've made things easier to swallow. But the memories force me to relive the moments I'd most like to forget.

The boy in the woods who did unspeakable things to me.

The monsters in the dark who paid for my flesh.

The blue-eyed savior who took away my pain.

When my thoughts turn to him, I ache all the worse. Someone may as well drive a knife into my stomach and twist the blade. I might fare better that way.

For all the darkness I loathe, the one I live in is warm and soft. It's not scary.

Yet, it has become its own prison. One I regularly try to beat against, to break the bars down around my mind.

The emotions follow the memories. Heartbreak and

fear and sadness. They knot and roll inside me. I'm scared the emotions will swallow me whole, drag me deeper. And then who would I be?

Who am I now?

The sounds hurt the least. It's the rush of the ocean, or distant crying. A shushing noise, over and over. A steady beeping. A breath.

The memories and emotions are my constant. They play on repeat. But the sounds ground me.

They're ever-changing, reminding me that I am alive.

I think I'm alive.

If this is Hell, I don't know what I did to deserve this place. I don't know what this eternal darkness has in store for me.

Is it a penance I pay?

A debt owed?

My thoughts wander until the noises finally shift. Until it's just a single voice cutting through the black, through the pain, through my growing fear.

A woman. She weaves me the most wondrous, hideous tale of love and heartache.

I want to take her hand and tell her that everything can be okay. But who am I to be optimistic when I'm trapped in Hell?

She might as well be right alongside me.

So I listen. And I remember.

And I hope.

In the end, that's all I have left.

1 ARTEMIS

SAINT IS INFURIATING.

I knew this about him, but I had forgotten. I mean, the guy knows how to pull at my heartstrings with the best of them. But in the blink of an eye, he's gone back to the self-absorbed, grief-stricken *asshole* who first moved into my condo.

He refuses to look at me. Or talk to me. Or be in the same room as me.

It's made our group therapy *so* enjoyable. He lasts only a few minutes before something sets him off. The sound of my voice, perhaps, or the way my gaze lingers on the side of his face?

None of this is my fault.

Not the stupid car accident that knocked common sense—and, okay, the memory of the last two years—right out of his pretty skull.

Not my delivery of his first love's death. Although, sure, it wasn't the best timing.

And it's definitely not my fault that he's trapped here with me, or that I can't stop staring at him. I mean, the guy told me he loved me, and now he hates me. What am I supposed to do with that?

Should I shelve my feelings now that I'm literally stuck on this island with him?

I'm *trying*, damn it. I'm trying not to care, but every time I see *his* face, or hear *his* voice, it sends little spasms of pain through my heart. Worse than the withdrawal, worse than craving heroin.

Him being here makes me want to swim through the icy water, back to Sterling Falls, and find Gabriel. To bare my forearms and beg him to just *please* put me out of my fucking misery.

Because that's what Saint is. Misery incarnate.

Those facts don't stop him. Actually, I don't think he registers my feelings at all. Like right now, the hallway practically vibrates with shocked silence. He saw me coming, amidst a crowd of fellow patients, and froze. Then, he spun on his heel, barged past someone, and tore outside.

In the middle of winter.

Without a coat.

If I didn't care, I wouldn't care.

That makes sense.

I just care so damn much, I want to strangle him.

So I hurry back to my room to grab *my* coat, then follow him. The fresh snow makes it easy. His footprints are clearly visible. He's heading in the direction of the dock. Like someone will be there to pick him up?

Or maybe he just wants to chuck himself into the ocean.

The wind snaps at my clothes, and my shoes are soaked through in seconds.

Damn him.

I keep going, though, because as much as I want to fucking strangle him, I also don't want him to die.

Mary Catherine, one of the other people staying on Isle of Paradise for the trauma center, whispered that any hint of suicide will mandate a twenty-four-seven watch until he's clear.

And I think that would actually kill him.

So I've kept it to myself, and he's wisely kept his mouth shut, too.

Finally, he comes into sight. The gray zip-up sweatshirt and sweatpants combo really doesn't stand out easily in the snow, amidst bare trees. Some pines held on to their dark-green leaves, but not many.

I open and close my mouth. If I yell for him now, there's every chance he'll just freaking increase his pace. Walking—eh, stomping—through the snow is one thing. *Running* is another.

The urge to call to him, though, bubbles up in me anyway. I lock my jaw against the desire.

He goes out onto the dock, exactly as predicted. I stop at the top of it, blocking his escape, before I make a noise. My cough is just loud enough to be heard over the ocean and wind.

He whirls around, and immediately, his eyes narrow.

Sterling Falls is straight across from this dock. If he

were stupid enough to jump, he could swim the distance. Ten miles, maybe? Just close enough to see the barest hint of light on a clear night. If it was summer. In the winter, he'd get hypothermia in a minute.

Right now, the sky is full of clouds that seem lower than usual. Someone mentioned it will snow every day this week.

The ocean is calm, though. Calm and dark, rolling softly under the dock.

"What do you want?" he spits.

My heart does that weird thing. Clenching tight, trying to cover over the hole he keeps tearing open.

I force a sigh and keep my expression passive. "To keep you alive, asshole. Hard to do when you can't even remember your coat before your winter hike."

He sneers. "I'm perfectly fine."

"Because you're numb on the inside and want to be numb on the outside, too?" I step forward. "You'll lose a finger. And then, when your memories come back and you remember what you did with Starlight, you'll realize what a giant fucking idiot you are. Risking your hands for—for—*this*." I motion, as if to encompass all of him.

"Starlight," he says carefully. "I kept it?"

Of course he kept it. Did he think he got rid of it? Does he have such little faith in himself? Unless he's considering quitting tattooing *now*. This is round two of losing Nyx, after all, and it was so much more abrupt. He woke up in the hospital and forgot that the love of his life was dead. He was lying in that bed expecting her to walk through the door, and reality bitch-smacked him. Now he's trapped on an island with *me*.

Maybe he doesn't want to do anything.

My brother and his two best friends pulled Saint out of the hole last time. They did a lot more for him than I ever could. I just took over and kept him alive by watching him.

Watched pots don't boil—and my job was to make sure Saint didn't boil over.

But it hurts, like a vicious stab wound, to think he would consider never putting his art on another body.

"You made it famous." I risk another step. He's in the middle of the dock, not in danger of suddenly pitching himself into the water. "Your face has been on magazines. Rich people travel to your shop."

"Right."

"What, you don't think you could do it?" My tone has turned sharp, goading. Begging him to admit that he thinks he's a failure.

Which for Saint is something he was never able to admit. Not in the beginning, at least.

The memory of him telling me he was attracted to me from the start, that *I* was his temptation, floats unbidden to the front of my mind. I bat it aside and focus on his scowl.

He shakes his head and turns away.

"Saint."

He doesn't reply. From the stiffness in his shoulders, to the tensed cords of muscles in his arms, his stance... he doesn't want a fight. He's bracing for impact.

At least before, I got his anger in my face.

"Saint," I repeat.

It isn't until I get close and grab his arm that he moves. He faces me, and his expression morphs into something awful. Angry, yes, but also horrified. Ashamed. Disgusted. I see it all bursting there, one after another, like fireworks. Each *pop* of emotion burns into my retinas.

If I didn't know him half as well as I do, I wouldn't be able to tell. I don't think I'd be able to read Saint Hart at all.

But I do know him, in all the intimate, impossible ways he can't remember. The slide of his palms over my breasts. His mouth at my neck. His cock inside me.

He grips my arms, and I don't even flinch, because he's finally fucking touching me.

Until he shoves me.

Shoves me.

I should've seen it coming. Shoulda, coulda, woulda. The problem is, I didn't. I wouldn't have imagined Saint ever laying his hands on me. It's not with malice. It's everything else twisting him up on the inside.

I should've predicted what comes next, too.

I slip off the dock and fall headfirst into the ocean.

2 SAINT

MY HEAD IS KILLING ME.

My mind keeps churning, spitting out cherished memories of Elora. And then confusing thoughts about Artemis. And then back to Elora.

Like how I tattooed her for the first time, close to the beginning of Olympus. When she became a regular fighter, and I started designing masks for Jace, Apollo, and Wolfe, we were free. We moved in together. I opened Starlight with the money from Olympus.

Dreams were happening.

But then the next moment, it's not Elora I'm tattooing, but Artemis.

I slam my palm to my forehead and try to clear the thought.

Antonio and a guy I didn't know came to the hospital after I screamed at Artemis to leave. I'll never forget her expression when I asked for Elora.

Heartbroken.

Her face shouldn't be familiar. It wasn't familiar, not really. I only knew of her as Elora's friend and Apollo's twin sister.

That's it. She was no better than a stranger.

And yet... something in her expression hurt me, too.

When Antonio and the stranger, who introduced himself as Reese Avery, asked if I wanted to go somewhere safe to heal, I somewhat readily agreed. It was better than going back to a life I didn't know.

They failed to mention *she* would be here.

Isle of Paradise is both familiar and strange. It seems to exist in its own reality. It's a comfort to be away from Sterling Falls. Outside of the most haunting memories. Maybe I'm imagining it, but there seems to be a cavernous void in my mind, and all the *old* memories—of Nyx, of happiness—bounce around.

But *Artemis*.

Everywhere I look, there she is.

Even when I most desperately need to be alone, she finds me.

I soak up her words about Starlight and try to imagine that I could keep existing after Elora died. I must've—I'm here. I've seen a calendar. Reese Avery showed me his phone, and the date on the screen was undeniable.

Starlight flourished in my grief.

And I...

I seem to have been through a war. I have more scars than before, including an hourglass-shaped one in the center of my chest. Bruises everywhere from the accident, although it's hard to see with all my tattoos.

Most of them, I'm familiar with.

There are a few new ones, though.

Like the little scales of justice on my upper thigh. It looks like my work, which is crazy. I've tattooed myself before, of course. But it's generally not my favorite thing to do. It's other artists' work that I want on my skin.

I don't know why I picked the scales. They're even, and each one has a flower on its plate.

Artemis grasps at my arm and pulls me from my wandering mind. Her hand on me, even through my sweatshirt, is like a branding iron.

I whirl around, and it's not hate that rises swiftly inside me, but something closer to craving.

Which cannot happen.

Not now, not ever.

I push her. Just to get her arms off me.

But the dock is icy, and her face immediately conveys her surprise. She slips, and she hits the water before I can stop her.

Fuck.

The fabric shoes issued by the center are the fucking worst. The walk here soaked mine, just as surely as they did hers, and all it did was make it easier for her to lose her balance.

Because I fucking *pushed* her.

It's freezing out—the water has to be worse.

Without waiting, I jump in after her.

Yep. Ice water surges over my head, and my muscles automatically lock up. This dock is meant for boats—it's already deep here, a few yards from shore. I open my eyes in the dark water and force my body to move.

I angle down and kick, searching for the feel of her.

My fingers touch something soft. It slips through my grip.

Deeper still.

Finally, I feel her hair. Then her head, her neck. I grab her by the upper arms and surge for the surface. My lungs burn, my muscles scream. Everything in me needs to save her.

If she dies, Elora will never forgive me.

We breach the surface, and I hoist her into my arms. I angle her head so it's propped on my shoulder.

Her skin is nearly blue. Instead of going for the dock and struggling to get her onto it, I swim us to shore. Drag her through the fresh snow until she's out of it completely. I put my fingers to her throat. They've nearly gone numb, but her pulse taps at them.

Her heart beats.

I watch for the rise and fall of her chest, only to realize that there is none.

She's not breathing.

I can almost hear Elora's voice in my head saying, *Mouth-to-mouth, idiot.*

I pinch her nose and press my mouth to her cold lips. Another flash surfaces of kissing her so hard, my heart felt like it was going to explode.

The concussion is messing with me.

I blow into her mouth.

Once, then again.

Her body convulses, and water comes up her throat, out of her mouth. She coughs and gags, and I roll her onto her side. She expels the remaining water from her lungs.

But she's *blue*.

And she doesn't wake up.

Fuck.

I peel the wet coat off her—it's probably the reason why she didn't immediately surface. It's *heavy*. She flops, completely unconscious, as I get her arms out. And then I lift her into my arms.

Why does she fit so perfectly?

With her head against my shoulder, her wet hair strewn across her face, I just want to scream. At myself, mainly.

I run back to the trauma center. Banging through the doors, I'm met with shocked faces. And then, an eternity later, Dr. Hawthorne appears.

She takes one look at me and Artemis, soaked to the bone, and her face goes white.

"With me," she barks.

I follow without comment. My heart slams my ribs, and I hold her tighter. I've lost feeling in my fingers and toes, but I refuse to let her fall. Water streams off us. Her hair, our clothes. We leave a trail. My shoes—those blasted, stupid fucking shoes—squeak on the tile.

We get to the small medical wing, where a nurse quickly directs me where to put her. Except I can't uncurl my fingers. I can't seem to release her at all.

When the nurse approaches, I growl at her.

Like a wild dog. The sound just pours out of me, and I keep Artemis to my chest.

"It's okay, Saint," Dr. Hawthorne says.

We've had a few sessions.

I've only been here for two weeks.

I'm not ready for this.

The rapport she probably needs time to build, to get me to trust her, just isn't there. I want to snap at her, too, but she circles around the bed so she can face me. With the nurse at her side.

"We need to get you both looked at, all right? We need to warm both of you up. The faster we can do that, the better."

It makes sense in my head, but my body refuses to obey. Not until the nurse and Dr. Hawthorne make me. They carefully peel away my hands and tug her body from my grasp. She slides fully onto the bed, limp.

With a gasp, I stagger backward.

"Sit," Dr. Hawthorne orders, pointing to a chair beside the bed Artemis now lies on.

I drop into it without question.

The nurse must've paged someone, because three others come sprinting into the medical wing. One splits off and comes to me, dragging the curtain closed between Artemis and me. With her out of my sight, it's simultaneously more painful and easier to breathe.

"Undress," she says.

Wordlessly, I strip down to my briefs. They're wet, too, but there's no way in hell I'm going to flash some strangers. I don't know what they're doing to Artemis on the other side of the curtain, and it's fucking killing me. It isn't until she procures new clothes—identical to the sweats and white t-shirt I shed—and turns her back that I strip the last bit of fabric from my body. I change fast and clear my throat when I'm done.

The nurse turns back around and puts a heated blanket around my shoulders. She checks me over and eventually gives me a clean bill of health.

Guilt gnaws at me, and my gaze keeps going to the curtain separating me from *her*.

"Saint?"

I jerk.

Dr. Hawthorne rounds the curtain. "Can you tell me what happened?"

My throat closes. "It's my fault. She slipped and fell in..."

I don't blame the coat for being too fucking heavy. I don't blame her for trying to reach me.

I blame myself.

"It's my fault," I repeat.

The doctor frowns. "Because..."

"I went outside without my damn coat. I went out onto the dock. She tried to bring me back in."

She just keeps trying to reach me, even when I push her away. Over and over. When am I going to fucking learn?

"Saint?" Her voice drifts past the curtain. "Is he okay?"

A nurse answers, "He—"

I launch out of the chair and swipe the fabric out of

my way. Only her face is visible under the pile of blankets, but she's awake and trembling like a leaf. I swallow sharply and ball my hands into fists. There's color back in her lips, although the rest of her face is still scarily pale.

She's normally golden.

Glowing.

How do I know that?

Her expression softens. "I'm okay."

Her teeth are chattering.

"I didn't ask," I reply quickly.

She winces.

I step closer. "Don't try to save me, Artemis. It won't end well."

I watch her face.

It shifts as my words sink in. But she doesn't cower—if anything, I only provoke her. She struggles to rise, and if I cared—*I don't care*—I'd put my hand to her shoulder and keep her down. But touching her seems dangerous, so I just clench my fists and wait until the blanket has slid down her chest.

Bare chest.

My gaze drops without my consent. First to the tattoo blooming across her collarbone, black ink reaching for the ball of her shoulder.

Scales of justice.

Wildflowers.

It's my work. I'd recognize my design anywhere, even if I don't remember doing it. I can almost picture standing in front of her, my hand on her hip—

She yanks the blanket back up, but not before I also catch the glint of metal in her nipples.

"Your nipples are pierced?" I blurt out.

She rolls her eyes. "Y-y-you're so f-fucking dumb."

That stops me.

"You think I haven't d-done this song and dance with you, Saint?" Her shivering, chattering only seems to be getting worse. "You think anything that comes out of your mouth this time around, you haven't already said under worse conditions?"

What?

I've seen her nipples before?

I must've, if I tattooed her...

No, that's a lie. I could've done that with her in a strapless shirt, easily. It means only one thing.

You fucked Elora's best friend?

Self-loathing hits me like a sucker punch.

I did. Of course I did.

She swings her legs out of bed. Bare toes feel for the floor, then make contact. I sway toward her, then freeze, while she just laughs under her breath. She holds the blankets to her chest and comes right up to me. She has to tilt her head back to keep her gaze on my face.

"Don't go thinking we aren't inevitable, babe." Her eyelashes flutter, and her dark-brown eyes bore into mine. "Even with all the guilt trying to crush you from the inside out."

It's like she can see my soul.

And I think it makes me hate her even more.

3 ARTEMIS

I STAY in the medical wing until after dinner.

Mary Catherine comes to visit me for the meal, sitting on the end of my bed and regaling me with stories. Stuff she thought I'd miss in less than a single day, like dining hall gossip. Who sat with who, et cetera. Oh, and naturally, the newest rumors about me and Saint.

Because we can't just *know each other* from the outside world. There's speculation on why he hates me and why I stare after him with such longing...

"I don't," I interrupt.

She grins, unconvinced, but thankfully changes the subject.

When the doctor on call comes to release me, Mary Catherine and I leave together.

"Movie night," she says, hooking her thumb in the direction of the recreation room. "You coming?"

I shake my head. "Just gonna go to bed, I think."

She waves me off.

As soon as she's out of sight, though, I pivot and go exactly where I'm not allowed.

Sleeping Beauty's room.

Well, *Lyssa's* room. I should call her by her name. I knew her years ago—in a way. I met her when she was already unconscious, lured into the darkness by the drugs *they* used to hold minds hostage.

Once upon a time, I helped Gabriel and Lyssa get out of Terror... at a very high price. And it seems, thanks to Gabriel, none of us are done paying it.

But learning Lyssa Laurent is Kade's sister? I didn't see that one coming.

I slip into the room and shut the door softly behind me. She's exactly as I left her yesterday, her hair perfectly spread on the pillow. She doesn't shift in her sleep, doesn't so much as twitch.

Since Saint's arrival, I've made the unfortunate habit of sneaking in here frequently.

I don't think that's normal for people in comas. I've read about it. Asked some nurses. Patients in comas, or under medical sedation, can still react. They might pull at their intubation, scratch, squeeze hands.

Lyssa isn't on a ventilator. She doesn't need any assistance breathing. She doesn't have reactions.

She just doesn't wake up.

"Sorry I'm late." I drag my chair closer. "You'll never guess what happened today."

I have no idea if she can hear me or not. I hope she can, because otherwise I'll eventually have to admit—to either myself or someone else—that I've been talking into the void for weeks. About nothing in particular, really. I didn't want to tell her about Terror. She had it a lot worse than I did in that hellhole. So I ended up just talking about Sterling Falls in general. The town I love and seem to be quickly losing.

Talking is therapeutic. Some might say that *talk therapy* works. But those people probably wouldn't say that if they knew I was talking to an unconscious girl.

Sometimes I lean forward and take her hand, squeezing her warm fingers, just so she knows she's not alone. In case the hearing thing isn't working, and the reflexes are just... in her brain. I don't know. I'm not a doctor, I'm just winging it.

They keep her room kind of dark. There's a warm, dim light on behind her head, and they never draw the window shades. I saw a note on her chart about it. That the view must remain unobstructed at all times.

Since Lyssa was not awake when she arrived here, it's probably a wish from a family member.

So who was it? Gabriel or Kade?

Right now, the view is mostly black. There's the glow of lights through windows in other parts of the building, and spotlights on sensors that flick on for unknown reasons. The wind moving the trees closest, animals, a wandering resident.

My attention slides away from the window, back to Lyssa.

I fill her in on Saint's asshole behavior, both on the dock and then afterward. I wrap my arms around myself and try to forget the lingering, bone-deep chill. I half remember Saint rushing from the dock back to the center, winding through the trees.

"...but what I'm really curious about is what's happening in Sterling Falls." I sigh. "There was a bad guy, Ouranos, who apparently took over with his gang. They're called the Cyclopes, which is kind of funny because they're known for being very single-minded. The monsters in mythology, obviously. And you know who else is a Cyclops?"

I shouldn't tell her.

"Your brother, Kade." I grimace. "I don't know your relationship with him, to be honest. He mentioned you in passing... said something about medical bills. I think he was downplaying it. And, little did I know, he meant *here*. But the other person is someone you're more familiar with."

My stomach flip-flops.

Do I tell her?

It's too late, now. I've dangled it in front of her. It would be positively cruel to keep it from her, especially since she can't sit up and beg me to tell her.

"Gabriel," I breathe. "He's gone mad in your absence, Lyssa."

This is so fucked up. I'm talking to an unconscious girl. And, in my mind, she's taken the role of best friend.

"Honestly, I'm not really sure what to do here. Finding you seems like impossibly good luck on my end. Keeping you out of Kade's or Gabriel's reach would certainly suit my interests. And maybe yours, as well." I glance around at her room. Gabriel wouldn't keep her asleep, would he? He was wrecked... but he's demonstrated the ability to do the same. To me. To Reese. How far would he go to keep his reality intact?

"Where would I put you?" I muse. "I don't have the means to care for you. I tried. Years ago. I don't know if you remember that. Things were more... tumultuous back then. Everything was uncertain."

I did try. And, in the end, I fucking failed.

I lean over Lyssa. "Wake up, please. If you're there in the darkness, I'm here waiting for you. I promise, this world is a lot different than the one you left."

I squeeze her hand.

And she squeezes back.

4 KADE

REESE WALKS TOWARD ME, and I allow my gaze
to roam his body. Not in a sexual way, but in a concerned
way. He's been holed up in Sterling Falls, coasting under
my radar, for far too long. The sheriff has been most
unhelpful locating him. Antonio Greco and his family
have also gone underground, leaving no one.

No Olympians, no Artemis, no Hell Hounds
encroaching where they don't belong. No promised final
stand.

It's left the door open for Ouranos to move in.

The city isn't any worse for the wear. Not yet. But
West Falls residents now pay a *protection* fee. There are
blockades everywhere, at the entrances to the neighbor-
hood, interspersed throughout, and it seems like Ouranos
only wants to push farther east.

Slowly.

Creeping.

Like a black fog, he's crawling toward a total takeover.

The opposition he faces: the city council, law enforcement. The Hell Hounds, once he crosses into their territory.

Reese Avery will fight.

Jace King, Wolfe James, Apollo Madden—they're out unless they can get back into the city. Ouranos has eyes everywhere. Gabriel made sure they couldn't return.

But Reese... he should've escaped when he had the chance. There's no telling what Ouranos will do if he gets his hands on him. The leniency he granted me, the *risk* I took to get Reese out—wasted opportunity.

He's in a jacket, hat, jeans, boots. His hands are tucked into his pockets, and his breath puffs out when he stops in front of me. The knit cap obscures his blond hair, but there's no hiding his hazel-green eyes and the hard cut of his expression.

"You look okay," I say to him, leaning forward in my seat. "Are you?"

He makes a face and sits beside me. He shifts, adjusting, and kicks out his legs. "Did you ask me here just to check up on me?"

Same old Reese.

"So what if I did?" I question.

It's not the reason, but I don't think I can come out and say it. Not knowing where Saint and Artemis are is killing me. All I know is that a Cyclops hit Saint's vehicle, and he was rushed to the hospital... then nothing.

No discharge paperwork, no trail to follow.

It's like he vanished into thin air, and I know all about

that. I'm looking at the ghost I've been chasing for far longer.

"I tried to find you for two years," I point out. "And it led me here." Two years of *breadcrumbs*. There was practically nothing but rumors to keep me going. Rumors and, eventually, a solid lead. A string I grabbed on to with both hands.

"Ouranos brought you here," Reese snaps. "You can lie to yourself, say that it was all about finding me. Following the fucking clues I left you. But I didn't expect you to bring a whole army—"

"Reese." I bite my tongue to stop the apology.

Our relationship has always been complicated. From serving together overseas, to the rough transition back home, to... *this*. We each have our trauma. He thought he could atone for his sins by serving his country. I thought I could outrun my past in the same way.

From the very beginning, we were like brothers. Through thick and thin. He saved my life, and I've been struggling to repay him in the same way. Struggling with knowing that, on the brink of death, I was so fucking ready for it.

And then he dragged me away from that edge.

"I did odd jobs for the Cyclopes in Emerald Cove," he says quietly. "Did you know?"

My breath catches, and I shake my head fast. "When?"

"Before I came here. It was just... It was surface-level stuff. I didn't want to get sucked into the gang, and some of the guys wanted extra hands-on jobs. So they paid me to hold a gun and make sure no one snuck in through the back door—that kind of thing." His shoulders inch higher. "The longer I was around them, the more openly they talked. Lesser stuff, usually, until they started on about how the Cyclopes were going to move to Sterling Falls because the previous gang had been wiped out."

"*Reese.*" I pinch the bridge of my nose.

All this time, he was there? We were in the same city?

I was searching for him, and if I had only opened my eyes sooner—

"I don't know how Ouranos got to you, brother," Reese continues. "I don't know what he promised you."

"He promised me *you*," I bite out.

He tenses. His gaze stays locked on the ocean, the waves crashing to the sand in front of us.

I stare at the side of his face. "I was chasing your ghost, and I practically fell into Ouranos' arms. He saw straight through me. Gave me structure. And, yes, he promised me *you*. Just as he promised Gabriel..."

Artemis.

He tenses, like I had said her name out loud.

"Why did you ask me to meet you here?" He makes a show of looking around the abandoned boardwalk.

Bow & Arrow, quiet and closed down, is just down the block. The beach is deserted, but the weather is biting. There's a layer of snow on the sand. Tourist season is over, which is what makes Ouranos' plan so brilliant.

By the time the ground thaws, he'll have control over

the whole fucking city, and the people who flock to Sterling Falls for vacations will be none the wiser.

"I wanted to make sure you're okay." I rub my hands together. The cold has officially sunk in, and my fingertips are tingling. "Again."

"Your act of saving me... It didn't do much, did it? I'm still here. Still stuck trying to figure out how to be better."

"Better?"

"Than my past." He shakes his head carefully, his gaze finally cutting to my face. "And maybe that means stopping Ouranos on my own."

I reach for him, but he rises and steps out of range.

"You wouldn't help me, Kade?" His expression turns pleading. "Why are you so invested in him? Help *me*."

"Tell me where Saint is." I stand, too. "You can keep Artemis. But Saint—"

He shakes his head fast. "No. *Saint?* You're so focused on him, now? No."

"Why?"

"Just accept the no, Kade."

I grit my teeth. "I'll follow you. I'll find them through you."

He laughs. "Good fucking luck with that one."

He turns and walks away. Shoulders back, head tall. My throat tightens, my jaw clenches. I look to the ocean again, but all it does is remind me of Artemis.

Asking for Saint's location and not hers is some sort of cruelty, but it's all self-afflicted.

I almost follow him, like I just threatened.

Instead, I sit back down.

5 REESE

I STEP into Kora Sinclair's house. We've kind of taken the place over in the past few weeks, but it still doesn't sit right with me. Every time I enter, I feel like a trespasser.

Daniel Kline sits at the kitchen table with two laptops in front of him. He's a friend of Artemis and Apollo—and the rest of their group, I assume—but he left Sterling Falls after the *last* gang war. He was able to get back in after we got Artemis out.

He's been diligently working on tracking Ouranos and the sheriff. Honestly, though, my eyes glaze over when he talks about the technical aspect of it.

Hacking.

He's in Bow & Arrow's security system, which has cameras pointed at the exits and throughout the building. He's managed to get into the sheriff's cell phone as well as some other businesses' security feeds.

Ouranos, however, has proven to be harder to pin down.

Vittoria, Antonio's wife, is in the kitchen. My mouth waters at the smell of whatever she's cooking—something with garlic, I'd guess.

I drop my hat on the table and peel off my jacket, and Daniel pauses his frantic typing to meet my inquisitive gaze.

"Anything interesting to report?" I ask.

He smirks. "How was the meeting with Kade?"

"Uneventful." I narrow my eyes. "Was it helpful?"

I can't really put into words exactly how it felt to sit across from him. He's working with Ouranos... he wants to take over Sterling Falls. It's only a miracle they haven't broken into Bow & Arrow and delved into Terror.

"Let me see it." He grabs my jacket and paws at the pockets. He pulls out the phone he had given me earlier and plugs it into a cord protruding from one of the computers. "Looks like it was a successful connection. Congratulations, Reese, you now have a clone of Kade's phone."

One step closer to Ouranos.

"What did he want anyway?"

I just shake my head and drag out a chair. I can't very well say he wanted to *check up on me*. That sounds lame, even in my head.

Kade called Artemis' phone, which was forwarded to a new burner of mine. She couldn't take it to Isle of Paradise, so Daniel set it up to help keep our locations a secret. At the same time, we didn't want her brother or his friends to call and not be able to reach anyone.

So I answered his call, and it was only arguments

from Daniel and Antonio that this would *help* us that convinced me to go.

Kade let me name the place and time, and I showed up an hour early to scope out the empty boardwalk in North Falls. Then made him wait an extra twenty minutes before I left my hiding place and joined him on the bench.

Vittoria glances over at us, a small frown on her lips. I meet her gaze and shrug. I don't have answers. Just theories that I'm not ready to share.

"I've got a boat," Daniel suddenly announces.

I freeze. "What?"

"Well." He clears his throat. "*We*'ve got a boat. Coming here."

"Here, like..."

"It's not really ideal," he admits. "But there's a ladder that they can get close to and get up the cliff."

"Who?"

He frowns, like I should already know who he's talking about. "Jace, Wolfe, and Apollo, obviously. And Kora, I suspect."

I wonder if they mind that we've moved into their house.

"When?" Vittoria asks.

"Within the hour." Daniel glances at me. "And if someone wanted to go visit Artemis on Isle of Paradise... We now have a way of getting there."

My gut churns, and I nod once. My throat closes, rendering me effectively mute.

Vittoria smiles. Just a little hint of one. "It'll be nice to have them back. Antonio is upstairs—Reese, could you tell him?"

I nod and point to the clone of Kade's phone. "Let me know if he uses it."

With Daniel's confirmation, I leave them and head upstairs.

We left the primary bedroom alone—it would've been really fucking weird for one of us to take their extra-wide bed—but there were a few guest rooms. Three, to be exact. Plus an office downstairs that can hold an air mattress, which wouldn't be off-putting since Daniel seems more inclined to do his work at the kitchen table instead of at the desk in the office.

I knock on Antonio's door and relay the message through it, then continue to mine.

I close myself in and lean my forehead against the wall. The blinds are still shut, the curtains drawn, and the room is dark. I blow out a long, slow breath.

If they're coming here... Perhaps I should borrow that boat and go visit Artemis. See how Saint is doing with the memory thing.

Make sure they haven't killed each other.

But how will Apollo, Jace, and Wolfe receive me?

Guilt swamps me. It's my fault that they left Sterling Falls. My favor that sent them to Emerald Cove, a timely mistake that could set them against me.

My favor—the person I asked them to free.

I haven't been entirely truthful with, uh, anyone. I

knew, almost two and a half years ago at this point, that Kade was keeping tabs on me. I was living a relatively normal existence, working a security job I hated, trying to grapple with what I saw overseas *and* my teen years.

And one day, it just occurred to me that I could fucking leave.

So I went to Emerald Cove, and I got looped in with the Cyclopes.

I met Ouranos.

Didn't tell Kade that, *did you?*

I met Ouranos, and I didn't buy the hype. In a way, he reminded me of my father. The type of guy who thinks the world owes him something. He spoke in fantastical ways, built an empire on selling dreams to his followers.

It seemed overreaching. Impossible—but not in a good way.

I was there when he found out his brother had been killed. I wasn't supposed to be—I was passing his office. But I heard him on the phone, promising to bring Sterling Falls to its knees for what that city did to his brother.

Still, I wasn't going to do anything. What did I care about that wretched place? It held Terror. It curated to the dark and depraved. Sterling Falls could rot.

But then I went on a job. One last job with the Cyclopes, and I met a girl.

A literal child.

She was more stuck than I was at her age—and that's fucking saying something. I tried to get her out, and it blew up in my face, and that's why I left Emerald Cove in a hurry.

Did they get her out?

Could they succeed where I couldn't?

I close my eyes and stay where I am until Daniel shouts about their arrival.

6 ARTEMIS

"I THINK you actually can hear me," I whisper in the dark.

Lyssa hasn't squeezed my hand again, and I had to leave before the nightly bed check. But once the coast was clear, it was easy to sneak out and back down here.

I go to the window. The moon is bright, the snow-laden trees casting shadows in the yard. In the distance, the water reflects the light, too.

"Maybe some fresh air will wake you up?"

There's only a portion of the window that slides, so I flick the latch and shove it open the designated six inches. It squeals, metal on metal, and I wince. Pause.

I glance back, just in case Lyssa flinched at the noise, but she's totally still.

Bummer.

Instead of returning to join her, I drag the chair closer to the window and prop my elbow up on the narrow sill.

The cold air that seeps in is welcome, even though the chill never quite left me.

Stupid Saint.

"*Fuck.*"

I straighten and slowly glance over my shoulder. The voice was distinctly male, and it came from outside. I stay perfectly still, unconcerned about being seen—the room is dark, with only the moonlight illuminating it—and wait.

Finally, a shadow seems to peel away from the tree line.

I tilt my head, the stride oddly familiar.

"How the hell am I supposed to find her?" His voice drifts toward me, clear and crisp even though it's low.

My heart skips.

I shove away from the window and bolt out of Lyssa's room without a word. I keep my footsteps as light as I can, but there's no stopping me from *running*. I skid around the corner and barely stop myself from slamming into the exit doors. The last thing I need is to get caught outside of my room.

My caution ends at making sure the door eases shut behind me, then I'm sprinting again. I round the corner and crash into a hard body. Hands grasp at my shoulders, easing me back, and I look up.

Reese Avery.

I blink, and he goes blurry. Tears fill my eyes and spill down my cheeks, and he immediately drags me into his chest. His arms band around my back.

"Oh God," I whimper. "You're really here?"

"Fuck, Tem, I thought it would be a whole hell of a lot harder to find you." His hold on me tightens.

His voice rasps in my ears, deliciously real. I inhale, my nose buried in his coat. His scent makes my heart ache.

"You okay?" His lips press to the top of my head.

"Yeah, yeah, I'm..." My throat closes. *Okay, so I'm not entirely fine.*

He guides my face up and brushes at the tears on my cheeks. His gaze takes in everything I'm not saying, and there isn't an ounce of pity in his expression. He has a bit of scruff on his cheeks. And circles under his eyes. His hair is hidden by a knit cap, but bits of it poke out around the edges.

It got longer.

"Is there somewhere we can go to get out of this cold?" he asks.

Reese isn't going to magically spirit me off the island, so I suppose suggesting the boat he came in on is out of the question. I step back slowly, but before I can retreat out of reach, he snags my hand in his.

An unexpected blush blooms across my cheeks, and another feeling shoots straight between my legs.

Oh.

"Answer me this," he says suddenly. "When you initiated... were you high?"

His grip on my fingers tightens, like he can read my mind.

"Please don't leave, Tem. I just—"

"I was." I shake my head. "God, I'm sorry I did that to you."

I didn't think about how it affected Reese. Or Kade, even. My actions didn't directly harm them, but it doesn't mean there's no hurt. My choices with them, *around* them, are a reflection of my state of mind.

Which was impaired.

"Can you forgive me?"

"Done."

I glance around, then put my hand to his chest. I guide him backward, into the trees, until he bumps into a thick trunk. I meet his gaze. "I'm not high now."

"No," he agrees.

"Never been more sober."

He doesn't stop me from slipping down to my knees, but his jaw works. His gaze stays glued to my face. I shove his jacket up, undo the button of his pants, and free his stiffening cock. It sways, pointing straight at me.

My mouth waters. I'm attracted to Reese. *Obviously.* I like his cock. But there's also an intimacy in being faced with it again that only comes from practice.

And, yeah, I know that the *practice* was in the worst spot imaginable, but he was a safe haven. He came to be one anyway.

I lean forward, opening my mouth and taking him into it. He lets out a faint groan. I put my hand on his stomach and push him back against the tree trunk. Once more of his weight is supported, I begin.

My mind swirls through lust, burning at the thought

of him coming for me. In both senses. He *came* here—and he's going to *come* in my mouth.

I take him deeper, working his length with my tongue. I know what used to make him explode, what moves used to make his legs quake and his hips jerk. He hits the back of my throat, and I barely suppress my gag.

Maybe I'm out of practice.

My cheeks hollow as I bob up and inhale through my nose. His fingers tangle in my hair. The strands slip through his grip, and his nails scratch at my scalp.

I hum.

"Ah, fuck," he groans. "Don't do that, I'll—"

Come too soon?

I suppress a smile for when I don't have a dick in my mouth. The snow crunches beneath my knees. I take him back in deeper, pressing my limits. Choking myself on him.

He fists more hair, pulling me back slightly. Then, pushing down.

My body sings when he takes control. The pulse of desire for him between my legs kicks up, but I force my hands to stay away. I want to *feel* it. To live in it for a while. The tingle of arousal, the rush under my skin.

I bob and suck, flick my tongue at the spot just under his tip that never failed to make him writhe. His hips buck, but he never yanks the control away from me. His hand on my head is a guide for what he wants—not a demand.

Not an order.

He lets me play with him, work him higher, until

every move has his hips rolling. He goes deeper, and I let him.

"I'm gonna come," he rasps. He tugs at my hair, as if to pull me off him.

I grab his ass and ignore the faint burn in my scalp. He's not *yanking*, not being cruel. But I don't let him move off me. I continue working him until his dick pulses. He moans my name and comes on my tongue.

I swallow it down, then slowly pull back.

That was, in a way, just what I needed.

And also, a whole lot less than what else I want right now.

I sit on my heels, my body buzzing. The urge to get myself off climbs but eventually passes. I exhale.

Reese slowly puts himself away, then helps me to my feet. His expression is dazed.

We just did that.

And, honestly, I have no regrets.

I wipe my mouth with the back of my hand, and it dawns on me how cold it is out here. Which reminds me of my recent discovery... and how Reese is probably the perfect person to tell.

I tip my head to the side. "So, um, I've got to tell you something."

7   SAINT

SLEEPING BEAUTY.

Why can't I get that out of my head?

I finished counting the cracks in the drop-ceiling tile an hour ago, and *sleep*, the very idea that keeps tumbling around my brain, still evades me.

It's better to consider a fairy-tale princess than the image of a very shirtless, shivering Tem.

No. *Fuck*. She's Artemis, not Tem.

Why do I keep wanting to call her *Tem*?

But onto a better question—who is Sleeping Beauty? One of the nurses mentioned needing to check on her, but it just seemed weird. So, naturally, I followed her down to the first-floor hallway and watched her disappear into one of the rooms.

Then, I retreated. I wasn't about to get caught snooping.

And in my mission to avoid Tem—*Artemis*—I returned to my room and stayed there.

Which is why I'm now awake, burning with energy.

I toss the blankets off my legs and slide my socked feet into the shoes set by my nightstand. By some luck of the draw, I don't have a roommate. The second bed sits empty, the mattress bare.

Moonlight comes in through the window, illuminating the small space. There's a desk and chair on my side, and a duplicate for my would-be roommate. My therapist suggested journaling, but so far all I've managed are a few letters I'll never send.

Because I'm apparently in the mood for pain, I open the top drawer and pull out the notebook. I shift closer to the window and flip to the last one I wrote.

DEAR ELORA,

You're dead.

The doc said I should say it plainly, because euphemisms won't help me. Saying you're gone or passed or that you've moved on—she's right, it's bullshit.

My tattoos are different. I've been trying to relearn them, in a way. Relearn my own body. The worst part is, I don't know what you've seen. The scar in the shape of an hourglass? Did you know that was there? Did you touch it before you died?

It marred some old ink, some tattoos I considered fondly. There were memories attached to those, just like the galaxy over my heart. I know, without any doubt, that the galaxy is you.

There's no one here to tell me what we went through.

The year gap I'm missing between you being alive and dying, then the gap between then and now.

Okay—there's one person. But I don't want to look at her face, because strange things keep happening to me when I do. My body seems to crackle with electricity, like lightning in a bottle. My heart picks up speed.

It's loathing. Unadulterated hate.

You have nothing to worry about.

Yours forever,

Saint

I GRIT my teeth and go to the next one.

DEAR ELORA,

You're right. I could practically hear you as I wrote the end of that last letter. I was lying through my teeth. But I need to lie to you about her, Elora. I can't bear to tell you that I'm experiencing some attraction to your best friend. You didn't agree to that, which makes it a betrayal.

I could ask Tem all about the time I'm missing, but I don't think I can stomach her answers. Or the hurt on her face.

Fuck, you should've seen her expression when she came into the hospital room and I asked for you.

She was listed as my emergency contact, but no one will tell me why. No one answers any goddamn questions around here. The doc says she doesn't know, that life beyond the island isn't written in her file.

And because I don't remember, I've been picturing the worst. I had a dream that your throat was slit, and I woke up crying. I scrubbed myself raw in the shower, washing imaginary blood from my hands.

That's wrong, right?

That's got to be wrong.

Because I also dream about her, *about the feel of her body and her fucking pierced nipples. Are her nipples pierced? I don't even fucking know. It's just the way I picture her naked, fully formed.*

I'm asking you these questions because you can't answer, and I don't want to know.

What I do know is, as jarring as this situation is, I fucking miss you. With every fiber of my being. I'd trade my life to get yours back. I'd walk straight into the underworld for you, Elora, and I'd carry you out even if I had to leave my soul behind.

A TEAR HITS THE PAGE.

I quickly close it and swipe at my face, embarrassment radiating through me. I'm crying? I cried when I wrote it, too, my vision blurring so much my handwriting got sloppy. There are already spots of smeared ink farther down.

Why did I dream about her nipples being pierced before I even saw them?

I hadn't realized.

Hadn't remembered.

And yet, today, I saw her tits, and there they fucking were.

I clench my jaw harder, until my teeth might crack, and put away the notebook. I can't stay here, pacing the room like a caged animal. There are night checks, but only once. They don't come back—and I don't think they patrol.

We're not prisoners.

My door is unlocked. There's no lock on it at all, actually. I grab my sweatshirt and slip out of the room, into the bright hallway. The light from the fluorescent bulbs overhead sear my eyes. I blink rapidly, checking that the coast is clear, then hurrying in the direction of Tem's room.

No.

Wait.

I pause at the top of her hall and shake my head. I am *not* going to her.

I'm going to satisfy my original curiosity about Sleeping Beauty.

Two minutes later, I'm outside her room. At least, I *think* this is hers. And I don't know why they call her Sleeping Beauty, unless maybe she has narcolepsy? This could also go really wrong if I enter this one and she wakes up screaming.

I might be committed to the *other* side of the island, where they do put locks on the door.

That's almost enough to make me turn away, but I catch a voice. Hushed though it is, it travels through the door and straight into my chest.

Artemis?

Okay, fuck it. Universe, you win.

Steeling myself, I grasp the knob and twist. I burst into the room, my finger already pointed in accusation.

But then, I freeze. Because she's not alone—and this setting is not what I was expecting in the slightest.

8 ARTEMIS

REESE IS CONFUSED, and I don't blame him. We went from blow job in the freezing cold to standing over an unconscious girl in her room.

"Lyssa Laurent," he says, repeating the name I told him not thirty seconds ago. His brows are furrowed, and he grips the plastic footboard at the bottom of her bed. "Laurent. Like *Kade* Laurent?"

"Half-sister, I think." I lean against the now-shut window. When we entered, it was a extra chilly in here—*oops, my bad*—and there are goosebumps on her arms. "But more importantly, she's Gabriel's..."

His gaze lifts to mine. "Gabriel's *what?*"

"Uh... First love? His deepest infatuation? Trauma-bonded soulmate?" I shrug. "Take your pick."

"Holy shit. And how do you know this?"

I shift. "Because I'm the one who got them out of Terror."

He stills. "That's not funny."

"It's definitely not funny. Terror didn't just dry up after my brother got me out. I made it my mission to end it, to save as many people as I could, but it still—" My throat closes. I swallow a few times, suppressing the sudden urge to cry, then finish, "It still wasn't enough."

Reese releases the edge of the bed and steps closer to me. "You got them out."

"And *this* was the price." I wave my hand at Lyssa's prone form. "I just—it wasn't ever my intention for Lyssa to be hurt when I was trying to help them. But it doesn't matter what my intention was. It happened. She's been like this for ten years."

Ten years.

"Artemis."

I shake my head. "Don't try to console me on this. The guilt I feel—"

"I can probably relate," he interrupts. "I know what being on the outside of Terror, and trying to right wrongs but being fucking helpless, does to a person."

I go quiet. He's right. I didn't want to think about that, about *his* side of things, but I believe in his character. I believe he didn't willingly go to Terror. And, as a sixteen-year-old, what power did he have to shut it down?

The image of him bursting through the door of one of the private rooms to get to me springs to mind.

"You became a sort of lifeline," I say quietly. When I walked into a private room and saw Reese, a tiny bit of the crushing weight lifted off my shoulders. "And what you were to me is what Lyssa was to Gabriel. He was trapped in Terror for far longer than anyone should've been. I can't even blame him for being what he is."

He opens his mouth, but I can't fathom what he's about to say. And he never gets a chance, because Lyssa's door suddenly swings inward.

Saint rushes in, his gaze immediately latching on to my face. Triumph—at catching me out of bed, in an off-limits room, perhaps—flickers across his expression, replaced immediately by confusion. His attention bounces between Reese, dressed in street clothes, to the prone girl in the bed.

Yeah, I'd be confused, too.

"Hey, buddy," Reese greets him, nonplussed by the unexpected intrusion. "You look better."

Saint narrows his eyes. "You came with me here."

Reese inclines his chin.

"Forgive me if I don't recall your name." Saint taps his temple. "The memory issues are a bitch."

Reese glances at me, then back to him. There's sympathy there, probably because Saint is being a dick right off the bat. For no fucking reason.

Welcome to Saint's world, Reese. We're all just existing in it.

Still, Reese seems unbothered. He smiles and introduces himself by name, then adds, "We're friends. And if you're going to gawk, you may as well close the door so we're not all ousted by orderlies."

Saint steps inside and lets the door swing shut behind him. It latches with a soft *click.*

The room shifts into an uncomfortable silence, until Saint finally gestures to Lyssa.

"Anyone going to fill me in? Or is this another thing I should know but don't?"

I cross my arms, moving slightly to block Lyssa's face. "What brought you down here, Saint?"

He scowls. "Why is every question met with another these days?"

"Oh, I don't know, because you don't do anything without a reason. And coming *here*, into *this* room, seems mighty suspicious." I glare at him. "What got you out of bed? Wasn't me."

Saint's nostrils flare. "You jealous, Tem? I'm coming to see some girl who isn't you in the middle of the night?"

I jerk like he hit me. A million responses bubble up in my chest, barely held back by the lump forming in my throat.

"Tell him," Reese orders.

I swallow sharply. *Tell him?*

He's not focused on Lyssa. We're not dropping back into the *who is she?* question. Reese wants me to address Saint's last one.

You jealous, Tem?

I slowly straighten my spine. The last thing I should be doing is cowering in front of *him*. I didn't cower when he was a feral animal trapped in my condo for a year. I met him head-on—with the truth. Or, some version of it.

This time can't be any different.

"I am jealous, Saint."

His eyes widen a fraction.

"I'm so fucking jealous that you are down here for some goddamn unknown reason, while I've been your personal punching bag *again*. And before that, just a few weeks ago, you were telling me you love me."

Saint's lips part.

Yeah, guess that one eluded him.

"You isolated prick." I approach him, and he goes backward. "You could've reached out to anyone back home. Jace. Wolfe. My brother. *Antonio*. Even Malik would've been honest with you."

"About?" His back bumps into the door he just closed.

"About *us*." I grip his white shirt in my fist, tugging slightly. "About me and you. About *you*. They could've told you a million stories of what happened to you between now and then. But no—you come here and terrorize me for some alleged crime."

"The only *crime* is my attraction to you." His gaze lifts over my head. Up, up, and away. "And my guilt for it."

Ah.

I release him.

Turn away.

We're back to that. Back to guilt, back to Nyx. She's still flesh and blood to him. Still real in a way I can no longer fathom. We lost her over a year ago, but he didn't.

"I told you a few weeks ago that I loved you," he says behind my back.

"Yes."

"It only took me a year to move on from her?"

The wobble in his voice shatters me. My vision blurs.

Reese acts fast. His hands slide up my arms, around my back, and he tugs me into his chest. I close my eyes, allowing him to hug me as the emotions rush through me.

I hate this part.

The part that instantly, viciously craves the drugs that can sweep these feelings away and replace it with a rush of euphoria instead. My skin crawls. My chest is hollow.

Finally, it fades. Like a tide receding, the need ebbs away. I take a breath, then another. Reese's cedar scent is familiar. Comforting.

"Okay," I mumble against his chest.

"Okay, golden girl," he murmurs, his lips in my hair.

When I glance over my shoulder, checking for Saint, my heart sinks.

He's gone.

9 REESE

TEM TAKES me back to her room. Sneaking through the shadows, keeping her close while hugging the wall, gives me strange flashbacks to my military training. I brush it aside and memorize where we're going.

Just in case I need to find her again in the middle of the night...

Or get her out of here in a hurry.

We go up a flight of stairs, and she hesitates outside of a closed door. Whatever internal debate she has is lost on me, and before I can ask, she turns the handle and steps inside.

I follow.

This room lacks the warmth of Lyssa's. The sleeping girl's room has so much *stuff*. Things that were sent by loved ones—who I now know is Kade, and maybe even Gabriel. When she wakes up, maybe she'll feel the power of that love.

Tem's room is painfully bare.

My chest pinches, and I have the urge to throw her over my shoulder and get her the fuck out of here.

This room is clearly meant to be a double. There's a bare mattress and empty desk pushed off to one side. Tem's bed is made, and some pens litter the desktop. There's a notepad of yellow legal paper, too, and it looks like some pages have been ripped out.

Things I don't question.

"How are things back home?" she asks, turning to face me. Her lower lip is trapped between her teeth.

I finally have her alone, and she wants to talk about home?

"How about..." I grab the desk chair and carry it to the door. I wedge it under the handle. "I strip you bare and show you how much I missed you, *then* we talk about Sterling Falls?"

Her eyes widen.

I tsk. "Come on, Tem. You didn't think I'd let you escape me so easily?"

She shakes her head. "Didn't expect anything."

"I'm glad we changed locations." I toe off my shoes. "Fucking in front of an unconscious girl would've been..."

Not cool.

Kinda cringe.

She laughs under her breath. "Yeah."

"Take your shirt off."

Her laughter dies, but she does what I say. She drops her shirt to the floor by her feet, then goes a step further. She folds forward, removing her sweatpants and panties.

Her shoes and socks go with it, kicked away to a pile with the shirt.

She straightens. Hands on her hips.

The moonlight is the only thing illuminating her room, and her back is to the window. The shadows hide the important details, like the curve of her stomach, her breasts. The bars through her nipples.

My dick stiffens, waking back up and tenting my jeans.

I move around her, and she shifts to face me.

The moonlight gleams off the nipple piercings. I want to touch her, but right now, she seems like a golden statue. Still, waiting, appraising. There's goosebumps on her skin.

She almost doesn't look like herself. She's missing the layers of necklaces, the makeup, the *fire*. Being here has dulled her, perhaps. Or just the toll of coming off the drugs. There are dark circles under her eyes.

"I need to see you, too," she whispers.

I nod. I peel off my jacket, then my shirt. My jeans and boxers follow. My socks. Naked, my dick pointing at her once again, I flash back to Terror. To standing in front of her. Waiting. Unsure. There as some sick lesson by my parents, some experiment to see if I'm twisted in the head.

Therapy would've been less traumatic.

"How do you want me?" Her husky voice goes straight through me.

I tilt my head.

"On the bed?" She goes back and perches on the

edge, slowly parting her legs. She doesn't touch herself, but I can see her arousal from here. "Like this? Or perhaps from behind..."

Another shift, and she kneels facing the wall.

No.

"Turn back around."

Her head drops for a moment, but then she does. She rolls, her legs still parted.

I grasp my length and bite back a groan. Now's not the time to be loud—our voices haven't risen above a whisper since we got up here. I'm aware of how thin the walls probably are.

A chair under the doorknob wouldn't stop someone from breaking it down to stop us.

I shake my head and pump myself slowly. "I don't want you on that bed, golden girl."

I pull the thin, flimsy mattress from the extra bed. It barely makes a noise hitting the rug-covered floor, and it'll save us from the giveaway of a headboard banging against the wall when I finally thrust into her.

She bites her lip again but drops silently to her knees. She crawls toward me, not stopping until she's planted her hands on my thighs and is once again eye level with my dick. She pushes my hand away from it.

I hadn't even realized I held it again, stroking it slowly.

She licks the precum oozing from my tip, just once, to make it twitch even harder.

"I'm burning up for you," I admit.

"Then come and take me." She shifts onto her back, propped up by her forearms.

Her gaze sears, and it's all the invitation I need to drop down to her level. I crawl over her, my body not yet touching hers. It will soon, in all the most satisfying places, but something holds me back.

I search her gaze.

"One hundred percent sober," she whispers.

This isn't a quick fuck with a girl I'm hot for. I notch myself at her entrance, still only a whisper of skin contact. She's wet, and it makes it easy to thrust inside just a little. The tip is swallowed by her cunt, and I let out a shaky breath.

I pull back and inch forward, testing my resolve.

Her muscles grip at me, but she doesn't even seem to breathe. She seems as captivated by the sight as me. When I stay still, her hips flex.

"Please get inside me right now," she begs. "This teasing shit is going to kill me."

I smirk. "Sorry, golden girl. Teasing isn't what I was trying to do."

I slide in deeper, inch by inch, until I'm fully sheathed.

Fuck. It's been too long. Weeks without has left me sensitive—I can only imagine how it's been for her. I doubt Saint has been helping her in that regard.

Or at all.

I bet *help* is a foreign word to him right now.

Knowing he had forgotten his shared past with Artemis is one thing—seeing his asshole behavior in person is quite another. Did her brother know how awful he was to her?

Her nails dig into my back, dragging my focus away from his treatment of her—and, ew, her *brother*—back to what I'm doing. Which is still, apparently, driving her nuts.

"More," she whispers.

I oblige. My abdomen ripples with every thrust, and I stay off her body enough to look at her. To shift onto one forearm and run my hand up her side and cup her breast. I brush my thumb over her nipple, tweaking the jewelry.

Her legs come up around me, and her heels dig into my ass. I lean down and kiss her.

Can't help it.

Maybe she wants a fast fuck, but I feel like I'm reacquainting myself with her after far too long. Her lips are still under mine for a moment, almost long enough to let a trickle of doubt in, and then she comes to life. She wraps her arms around my neck and draws me down.

My weight presses onto hers, chest to chest. Her mouth opens, allowing our tongues to meet. The kiss, the way she feels around my cock, the warmth of her body— it's all too much.

I could go back to thinking about her brother to hold off my orgasm...

Her teeth score my lower lip, and I groan. I roll my hips and hit a new position, and she whimpers.

Oh, fuck.

I chase that noise, repeating what I did before. I hit a spot deep inside her over and over again. She gives it to me. I take my hand from her breast and drift it down between our legs, feeling where I slide into her. Then up, to the bud of nerves just waiting to be touched.

Our kiss breaks off, our lips hovering, so close we're still nearly touching. I open my eyes to find her already looking at me. Her dark-brown eyes are wide. She seems younger without the makeup. More like an innocent twenty-five-year-old who hasn't been fucked over by the world on repeat.

Not that she looks like a harried old lady *with* makeup—this is just a kind of vulnerability I appreciate. Her makeup is a shield.

And right now, there's nothing between us.

No condom either.

Ah, shit.

That thought alone seems to trigger some insane bodily response. My balls tighten, and the pleasure that is natural to chase—the tingling forewarning that it's coming—starts at the base of my spine.

I pull out.

Try to anyway. But her heels keep me trapped, and her nails dig into the back of my neck.

"Tem, I'm not wearing—"

"I'm on birth control. Don't worry about it." She rises and captures my lower lip in her teeth again, tugging.

I'm a fucking goner.

I work her clit with my finger, and I thrust into her with renewed vigor, chasing the high of climax. Both of ours.

She breaks before me. Her back arches, pushing her

breasts into my chest, and her pussy clamps down on my cock. The sight of her unraveling, her eyes squeezed shut, her mouth open, does me in.

My head falls into the crook of her shoulder when I come, filling her up. My strokes turn lazy, slow. I milk out every last ounce of feeling, until I shudder and stop, resting inside her.

How am I supposed to leave her after that?

"Thank you." She strokes my hair.

Thank you?

"For?" My voice, muffled against her neck, is gruff.

"For not letting me suffer this place alone."

I let out a quiet chuckle. "Golden girl, I'm about to enroll here myself just to do this to you more often."

I don't say the thought that directly follows: that this place would absolutely beat the shitshow Sterling Falls is going through right now.

Instead, I keep my mouth shut. And I'll stay here as long as I can, wrapped in Tem's embrace.

10 KADE

I DIDN'T NEED Reese to find Saint Hart.

I found him myself.

Dr. Hawthorne shadows me down the hallway toward my sister's room. She is as put together as always, a steadfast presence that tracks my mannerisms with precision. She's always left me a little unsettled—probably because she gives off the air of someone who can *read* others.

That would be the psychiatrist part of her, I imagine.

Still, some secrets of the mind are better left uncovered. Knowing she can probably guess at reasons behind actions only makes me want to behave irrationally. To throw her off.

It's a bit ridiculous.

Anyway. Ouranos gave me leave to check on my sister, as I do every month. Gabriel came a few times, but we both noticed his behavior was worse upon returning.

Eventually, I stopped inviting him. The guy is unhinged as it is—no one wants to see him *worse*.

"How is she?"

Dr. Hawthorne clears her throat. "She's the same."

I pause long enough for her to catch up—the step-behind bullshit drives me nuts—and meet her gaze. "I know she's the same. I get regular reports from her doctor. Tell me more."

"A resident stole some things from her room, but they were recovered. She is regularly moved to prevent bed sores and put through physical therapy to keep her muscles from atrophying. Her feeding tube doesn't seem to irritate her. Otherwise..."

I narrow my eyes.

"Some residents like to visit with her," she admits.

"Why?"

She shrugs carefully. "I've heard they like talking to her. And, honestly, if they can open up *somewhere*, it's encouraged."

Anger sweeps through me at her carelessness. We're outside her door, now, and I point to it. "You let strangers go into her room? Without supervision?"

Her mouth opens and closes.

She's a psychiatrist, yes, but she also runs the facility. She knows the inner workings. It's why she met me at the dock this morning herself instead of sending someone else. Because I pay an exorbitant amount of money to keep Lyssa safe.

Safe in a way I failed as a teenager.

"Well?" I demand. "How am I to ensure my sister's protection if *anyone* can stroll into her room?"

Dr. Hawthorne nods. "You're entirely right."

Great.

I open the door, only pausing to glance back at her.

And that's when I spot Saint Hart.

The back of him anyway. But who else has his hair, his stature, and his *tattoos*? He wears a plain white t-shirt and gray sweatpants, the former doing nothing to hide the artwork on his arms or neck. His hair is cut short in the back, a fade into a slightly longer top.

"Mr. Laurent?" Dr. Hawthorne murmurs.

I focus on her, then back to Saint—and he's gone.

Damn it.

I shake my head and step into Lyssa's room. The flowers on the tables have been changed recently, the water in the glass vases clear and fresh. And she lies in the center of her bed, her hair brushed, her skin clean.

My heart skips.

I go to her side and take her hand in mine. I run my thumb across her knuckles. There's no change, no flicker of life in her expression—or in her hand. It's cool and dry, just like every other time I've touched her.

And, just like every other time, my stomach knots.

I release her and turn away, satisfied that she hasn't been left destitute—or, worse, that these other residents have been malicious. Outwardly.

"I want her skin inspected for bruises," I say. "And her door should be locked."

Dr. Hawthorne clears her throat. "Only a few of my

staff hold keys. That in itself is a safety concern, and not just for Lyssa. For this entire facility. And if something were to happen—"

A million scenarios flash through my head. A fire, and prone Lyssa trapped with no one there to help her escape. If she choked, if her heart stopped, if she somehow fell from bed or had a seizure...

I can't compromise that aspect of Lyssa's care.

I wave her off. "Fine. Let's discuss other measures, then. In your office."

I lean down and press a kiss to Lyssa's forehead, then sweep past her, back into the hallway. I scan it for signs of Saint and continue to do so on the way to the doctor's office. My gaze absorbs the lack of a computer on her desk. The discreet filing cabinet in the corner.

Paper filing system? I suppose that makes sense to prevent hackers... and they're on an island. Who's going to sneak onto the island to rifle through files in a locked office? The sheer number of obstacles in the way...

Plus, it forces would-be thieves to put themselves in physical danger, instead of hiring out to hackers.

It's smart.

It puts a damper on my plans to get off this island *then* figure out how Saint ended up here, but alas. I have no doubt an opportunity will present itself at some point during my stay.

Gotta admit, I sort of pictured Saint and Artemis holed up somewhere, scheming...

But Isle of Paradise wasn't on the radar.

Hmm.

"Mr. Laurent," Dr. Hawthorne begins.

Almost immediately, her phone chimes twice. It's followed by a low tone that echoes from the hallway.

She was halfway seated, but now she rises. "I'm so sorry. Can you excuse me for a moment?"

She's out the door before I can muster a response. I wait a few seconds, then poke my head out the door.

The corridor is empty.

See? Opportunity.

I round her desk and test the cabinet drawers. Locked, as suspected. A quick perusal of her desk supplies me with the tools I need, and in under a minute, I'm into the top one.

Another minute, and I scowl. I do not understand her filing system. It wouldn't be *easy* if it was just in alphabetical order by last name, but this seems to organize her patients—or, as she calls them, *residents*—by some sort of coding. That's the part that doesn't quite make sense yet.

I do enjoy a challenge.

My ears strain to catch any sound from beyond the office. It wouldn't surprise me if the room was soundproofed. Behind me is a couch and chair, presumably for private sessions.

The thought of her poking around in my head is almost as bad as knowing she's analyzing my body language and every facial expression. And my language.

I pull a file at random. It has a series of numbers on top, 26325, followed by a string of letters.

It doesn't correlate to anything in the girl's file.

There's not even a picture attached. Maybe that's in a database somewhere, or—

Who fucking knows.

I drop it back in. The pressure of *time*, of getting caught, beats down on me. I close and relock the drawer, returning her implements to their proper places, and sit back down.

Not a second later, the door opens.

It's not Dr. Hawthorne, though.

It's just the man I was hoping to find.

Without thinking, I smile.

Thank you, Opportunity.

11 ARTEMIS

TWO MAJOR FUCKING PROBLEMS.

One—Kade Laurent is *here*. On Isle of Paradise. I barely had time to hide in Lyssa's room, sort of proving his argument with Dr. Hawthorne correct about *anyone* coming in. There aren't a lot of places, so I dove under her bed right as the door opened.

I overheard their conversation, but he didn't linger. I focused on his shoes right at the edge of the bed. Working boots, jeans. Not the sort of thing Atlas, his Olympus alter ego, would've worn. The lower half of him reminded me more of Reese than anything else.

And that brings me to problem number two—Reese didn't leave.

I woke up to him curled around me, and panic thrashed in my chest that we were going to get caught. I elbowed him awake, then left him to get dressed while I used the attached bathroom. When I reemerged, he was dressed but fucking sexy with his sleepy eyes and messed hair.

"What are you doing?" I hissed at him. "You were supposed to go—*hours ago*."

He waved me off. "Relax, golden girl. I paid for my slip at the marina on the town side."

After that, he went out the window and promised to return later.

But now, I'm panic-searching for Saint. Saint will not recognize Kade, but the opposite isn't true. In fact, Reese mentioned, sometime during the post-sex haze, that Kade specifically asked about Saint.

Fuck. Fuck me.

Why is Saint Hart the most difficult person to find?

"Tem!"

I pivot. "Mary Catherine!"

"You're flushed." The girl stops in front of me, her hands in her pockets. "You okay?"

"I'm looking for Saint. He's giving me the runaround."

Her eyes widen. "Oh, no. Is he avoiding you after the whole push-you-into-the-water incident?"

"Um..."

"There was an issue with one of the other residents." She loops her arm through mine and steers us in the direction I was heading. "Dr. Hawthorne seemed to think they'd need sedating. Only the most dramatic get the shot, but that guy was wailing. It was an awful sound."

I roll my eyes. "Okay...?"

"Saint was there."

"Where?"

"In the cafeteria." The *duh* is implied. "And I'm pretty sure he asked if Dr. Hawthorne was going to be late for their therapy session."

I stop.

Mary Catherine's arm slips from mine, and she belatedly turns to face me. "What?"

Dr. Hawthorne is an *idiot*.

I shake my head and burst into a run. Up the stairs to the second floor, down the hall toward her office. I know the route well. I get there just as Dr. Hawthorne appears from the opposite direction. She marches with purpose, but her eyebrows lift when she spots me.

It takes me a second to control myself and slow to a walk.

"Dr. Hawthorne," I call. "Have you seen Saint?"

She frowns. "I—"

We reach her office door at the same time.

"Just in passing," she says. "We have a session, but I expected him to be in the hallway..."

"And I don't suppose you left Kade Laurent unattended *in* your office?" I whisper.

"How—"

I motion to the door.

She opens it, but my stomach is already twisting. I expect to see Saint and Kade sitting together, talking.

Instead, her office is empty.

"KADE?"

The name is out of my mouth before I can stop it. I clap my palm over my lips and duck behind a parked car. Luckily, he's too far away to have heard me. The town on Isle of Paradise is *tiny*. Like, one narrow main street with some shops and accommodations for the workers, but that's it. And a good amount of woods separates it from the trauma rehab buildings.

Kade strides purposefully down the sidewalk, toward the marina I just left. I went to pay for another day, to which the harbormaster accepted my money with a suspicious glare, and to check on the boat I borrowed from Tem's brother.

It's in fine shape.

But *Kade?*

I pop up to get another look at him once he's passed, and only then do I register the guy with him. Kade's black leather jacket slung over his frame doesn't hide the standard-issue gray sweatpants and slip-on shoes.

Or the tattoos.

Why the fuck is Saint going with Kade?

Does Kade have a gun trained on him?

I glance around, half expecting Artemis to be giving chase. But the street beyond is relatively quiet.

Isle of Paradise isn't exactly a tourist destination. Especially in the winter.

So that gives me two choices: I go back for Artemis, thus potentially losing Kade *and* Saint, or I try to catch up with Kade and reason with him.

Oh.

Wait.

Three choices.

I happen to have a secret specialty skill, and it will be perfect put to use and cause a distraction.

I make a beeline into the closest store and slap a fifty-dollar bill down on the counter next to the clerk. "I have a favor to ask..."

13 ARTEMIS

I END up telling Dr. Hawthorne more than I probably should. I pace in her office the whole time, in front of the couch, too upset to even consider sitting. My fingernails dig at my arms, the crooks of my elbows.

"Take a breath, Tem."

I still. "You want me to *breathe?*"

"You're speaking a hundred miles a minute, so, yes." She tilts her head. "I've already alerted the marina that someone is trying to remove one of our residents against his will. They will stop it."

I scoff. "You've *met* Kade Laurent before, right?"

She doesn't have a response to that. It's laughable to even think some guy locking the gate to the marina would stop him?

"Are you sending people to find Saint?" I ask her. "What if he stashed a boat on the dock closer to the center—"

"Artemis," Dr. Hawthorne warns. "Please."

"*Please?*" I laugh. "Do some fucking research next time. This place is supposed to offer safe harbor—"

"And it does—"

"Yeah, until one of your donors comes calling and kidnaps a guy with amnesia!" I shriek.

I can't stay here for this. I exit her office and hurry to the first floor. I weave around other residents, most of which are now familiar faces, and speed-walk to the exit. Out the door, into the frigid air.

My pace picks up when Dr. Hawthorne shouts my name behind me.

I'm halfway down the trail when a sound like a canon goes off. A split second later, the ground shakes. I stumble and catch myself on a tree, staring in the direction of the sound.

A siren goes up through the air.

What the fuck?

Last year, my brother and I found a subway car packed with explosives. It was part of a takeover plot, and we barely made it out of there without detonating it. That sound—the way the force of it shook the ground under us—feels an awful lot like this.

Fear kicks my body into overdrive. I sprint down the trail, bursting off the path into the town. *Everyone* is outside. Visible over the buildings is a plumb of smoke rising into the air. Forced to go slower, I head in that direction. A firetruck turns onto the main street ahead of us, blasting its horn to get people to move. The vehicle looks like it's two decades old.

Murmurs follow me. There's a slight stigma about those of us who come for... *rehabilitation.* The trauma center funds the island, but alas. It apparently doesn't matter all that much when the residents have a variety of quirks.

This street funnels to the small marina. I'd bet most of the townsfolk have their own boats, and Reese had docked here.

Wait.

Shit, Kade, too?

The smoke makes it clear that it wasn't a building that exploded. It's too far out. Maybe a boat caught fire and the gas tank made that noise? It would be possible... it could've been a bigger ship. Possible. *Plausible.*

I finally clear the buildings and stop short.

Wishful thinking on my part.

The whole fucking marina is gone. There are some boats in the distance, seemingly unmanned and being pulled out to sea. Ropes trail off their sides in the water.

But the *docks,* the fencing that kept people out, and the boats kept close—as well as the harbormaster's office —have been obliterated.

How?

Why?

Unease slides through me.

Was this Kade?

Or... Gabriel?

Gabriel tried to blow up Terror. It would not be out of the question to assume he'd followed Kade, spotted me, and wanted to trap me here.

Is that a *little* egotistical to think everything is about me? Probably.

But *damn*.

The firefighters are busy putting out lingering flames, but there's not much to salvage. A crowd gathers around me, spectators drawn to the sight. There's tension in the air. Some whisper about accidents, others suggest terrorism. But who would try to terrorize the Isle of Paradise?

"This will take weeks," someone murmurs. "There's that other dock, but I imagine it'll be under supervision."

"Whose?" another questions.

"I imagine it would be a Coast Guard problem. And then, if this wasn't an accident, there will be an investigation..."

A chill runs down my spine.

I slip away. I didn't grab a coat, and the thin, long-sleeve shirt isn't cutting it now that my adrenaline has worn off. I glance down an alley on my way back and freeze.

Saint.

But, worse—Kade. He has someone pinned to the wall, and my heart skips.

Fucking Reese.

I don't think about it. I immediately change direction and approach them.

"Are you following me?" Kade asks, shaking Reese by the front of his shirt.

Reese, for his position, seems largely unbothered. "You'd be so flattered by that, wouldn't you?"

Neither man notices me. I come to a stop next to Saint, whose cheeks are flushed from the cold. He looks over, and his eyebrows rise.

"Don't seem so surprised," I whisper. "What the hell are you doing?"

"This guy presented an interesting offer."

Oh, jeez. "Did it involve his dick?"

He stiffens. "Excuse me?"

"I thought we met in good faith," Kade seethes at Reese. "But you had an ulterior motive, huh? Bug my phone—"

Reese laughs in his face. "You used to be more creative. *Good faith?* You've been around Gabriel too much."

"Who's Gabriel?" Saint asks me.

"Lyssa's..." I shift. "Lyssa's Nyx, I guess."

His lips flatten. I imagine he might put together the pieces—Lyssa being unconscious, Gabriel out there in the universe. But then he might ask, where does Kade fit into the equation?

"Gabriel is also somewhat psychotic." I elbow Saint. "Good thing you didn't go that route."

Saint snorts. "I still could."

Yeah, you could.

Reese and Kade are still arguing.

"Does Kade know I'm here?"

Saint looks down at me and frowns. "How would he know?"

"Did you say anything?"

"I walked into Dr. Hawthorne's office, this dude was there. He seemed *not* surprised to see me, so I figure we had met. But I'm not about to show all my cards. And he asks if I want to get off the island. Obviously I said yes."

He hasn't referred to Kade by name.

I slowly shake my head. "His name is Kade Laurent. Lyssa's brother. He was on the island to check on her, and I would bet twenty bucks he spotted you somewhere. But more importantly, you went with a stranger and you didn't *ask who he was?*"

Saint's cheeks get redder. "I didn't think giving away my vulnerability was a good idea."

Oh, for fuck's sake.

I smack his chest. He's wearing Kade's goddamn jacket.

"So, who set off the..." I gesture vaguely behind us. "And how did you guys find Reese?"

"Kade." Saint pauses. "Kade saw Reese on the street after. It nearly blew us off our feet."

"It felt big," I admit.

"That's what she said." He smirks.

"*Focus.*" This is the first time that Saint has been both forthcoming *and* not a sarcastic asshole to me. We need to keep the momentum rolling in the right direction.

"He thinks Reese set it off. I don't know why he'd suspect that, but I just followed after him. Gotta admit, I was curious about the guy. Comes in all smooth-talking, offers to get me out of here, and now this?" He motions to them. "Do they always fight like this?"

"No. I don't really know how they fight. I've only seen them bicker a few times."

Their conversation—Reese and Kade's, that is—has shifted away from the mess at hand to something in their past. Which seems a bit pointless, if you ask me. Off topic.

"Huh," Saint says.

I eye him. "What?"

"Did you rush out here after me?"

"Because I thought Kade was going to sweep you away and I'd never see you again?" I grimace. That's too close to the truth for my liking. "Don't flatter yourself."

"You're shivering," he points out. "Weren't you yelling at me about not wearing a jacket?"

I cross my arms. There are goosebumps on my skin that I do my best to ignore. From the street behind us, it sounds like the small local police force is clearing the streets.

I stride forward, within reach of Kade and Reese, and clear my throat loudly.

They both start. Reese doesn't seem surprised to see me, but Kade's eyebrows shoot up.

"As much as I'm enjoying whatever *this* is..." I gesture at Kade's grip on Reese's shirt. "We should get out of here."

Kade slowly releases Reese's shirt. He wears a fitted long-sleeve black shirt, also at odds with the weather. His hair appears recently trimmed. Reese takes one look at me and pulls off his coat. He offers it to me.

I'm not too proud to ignore it, so I turn and let him

slide it up over my shoulders. Then, wordlessly, he spins me back and zips me in.

Warmth—and his scent—envelops me.

"Where to?" Reese finally asks.

Kade scowls. "I would've said my boat, but you blew that up."

My eye twitches. *Reese* is behind it? No—he's going to deny it at any second. But then he doesn't.

Reese blew up the marina?

I smack him. "What is wrong with you?"

He points at Kade.

Well… that's fair.

"We should get off the streets," Saint says. "Like Artemis said."

I glance back at him, but he's focused on the mouth of the alley. The flash of blue and red lights from police cars paints the sides of the buildings on both directions. We really shouldn't be caught out here. Not when one of us is guilty of the crime.

"Kade should leave," Reese interjects. "You two should go back to the center. And I'll…"

"You blew up my boat." Kade crosses his arms.

"He said that already," I mutter. "And…"

How do I convey to Reese through mind-speak that *Kade* being here is actually probably better for us? We can get answers about the Sterling Falls takeover.

"This island is going to be on a full lockdown in a matter of hours," Kade says. He eyes Reese, then me. "If you wanted a way to keep me here, congratulations. You succeeded."

Reese grimaces. "I didn't want to keep *you* here."

I snort.

Saint's gaze bounces between us, his eyebrows up to his hairline. He's probably trying to figure out the dynamic—and, pre-amnesia, he would've added a whole new layer to it. Now, he's partially removed to observer.

"We can go to my house," Kade finally says.

My jaw drops. "Excuse me?"

His gaze meets mine—for the first time, he directs *all* of his attention to me. It burns, a million emotions in his expression. None of those emotions are malicious, though. Pity, concern... happiness?

Surely not.

"I bought a house here when I moved my sister to the island."

Okay, Kade. We'll pretend I have no idea who your sister is.

He tips his head deeper into the alley. "We can cut through this way."

I exchange a look with Saint, but he's useless. He scowls at me and throws his hands up as if to say, *What do you want from me?* I don't know, Saint, a little clarity? An opinion?

Saint doesn't give a shit about that, though, and sets off after Kade without hesitation.

Reese sighs. "May as well. He's not gonna kill us in our sleep."

I pause. I hadn't thought of *that* option.

"He's not." Reese holds out his hand to me. "He's

made a mess of your city, but I still do trust him not to stab us in the back."

"That's not very high standards," I mumble.

He chuckles. I take his hand, his warm palm against my chilled one. He tugs me into his side and kisses the side of my head.

"This could even be a good thing," he adds.

14 SAINT

THERE'S some interesting tension going on in this room.

I sit in an armchair, a mug of coffee pressed between my palms. I have phantom sensations lingering in unexpected places, which is pulling some of my attention. Mainly the ghost of Kade's hand on the back of my neck.

We were just approaching the marina when the whole thing went up in a fireball. I was walking shoulder to shoulder with Kade, whose name I didn't know at the time. I was going to figure that out sooner or later. It just didn't seem *particularly* important when he seemed happy to see me. And then he offered to get me out of here.

Who was I to refuse?

But *no*. The marina exploded, and Kade reacted quicker than me. He grabbed me by the back of the neck and dragged me down to the sidewalk. It happened too fast to register, but then the air settled, and all I could feel was his fingers digging into my skin.

My face heats, and I scratch at my throat.

Artemis is the only familiar one. My gaze stays stuck on her, perched on the edge of the couch like she's ready to bolt. Her mug, supplied by Kade, sits forgotten on a side table.

Reese is over by a bookshelf, scanning titles.

I don't know where Kade is. This place is less *house* and more *cabin in the woods*. It's a vibe, to be sure. Probably not *my* vibe... definitely not Tem's, judging by the way she seems stressed out.

There's a minimal amount of dust on the surfaces, inferring that Kade probably has a cleaner out here a few times.

"We should go back," Artemis finally says.

Reese glances at her. Can he feel how thick this tension is? I can cut it with a knife—and its sole source is *her*.

"Where did he even go?" she hisses. "He could be calling in backup—"

"I went to get firewood," Kade rumbles from the entryway.

He toes the thick door shut. His arms are full of chopped wood, which he deposits on a metal rack by the fireplace. He crouches, giving the room a view of his ass, and starts to build a fire.

Do I know how to build a fire? No. I know how to put one of those ready-to-go logs in and light the edges, but that's about it. My Boy Scout training stopped there.

Artemis lets out a huff and settles back in her seat. "This is ridiculous."

"You're telling me." Kade peeks back. "I was just—"

"You were trying to kidnap Saint!"

I take a sip of my coffee. Was that what Kade was trying to do? *Scandalous.*

Kade scoffs. "I was offering him a way off this island, since you decided to hide—"

"That's rich." Artemis throws up her hands. "You walk into a situation half-cocked, like always—"

"I don't do anything *half-cocked*," Kade interrupts.

A blush blooms across her cheeks. She presses her lips together for a moment, then shakes it off. "You don't know anything."

"You're right." He rises and faces her, but all it does is position him to tower over her seat.

Never one to back down, she stands and pokes her finger into his chest. Their size difference is comical. Not because Tem is short—she's average for a girl—but because Kade is so massive. He's got a few inches on me, even.

"I know I'm right," she says through her teeth.

"All I *know* is that Saint was in a car wreck, then he disappeared."

Reese clears his throat. "And you know that because you were meeting with him?"

Artemis jerks like Reese prodded her with a fork. She turns to glare at *me,* although I think we've established that I have no fucking idea about any of this. I shrug at her, but it only seems to pour gasoline on the flames. Her face reddens, and she whirls back toward Kade.

"Why were you meeting Saint?"

Kade raises his hands in surrender. "I never actually met him that night. Not sure where you're getting your information, Reese."

Artemis growls. "Will you *ever* just tell us the fucking truth?"

He pauses. *Considers.* I can see the wheels turning, and I hate to say that I'm just as curious as him. I was going to meet him that night? And apparently got in a wreck along the way.

Does that mean *I* trusted him?

"Ouranos took an interest in Saint."

A chill sweeps down my spine. That sounds fucking ominous.

"He asked me to..." Kade clears his throat. "Find him."

Artemis narrows her eyes. "Why did he take an interest in Saint?"

Kade, to my utter shock, blushes.

"Before we go admitting to stuff, we should all remember that Saint has no idea what's going on," Reese interjects.

I lean back in my chair. I hadn't realized I was so far forward, my interest piqued. What's with the blush staining Kade's cheeks? What is this dynamic?

Also, am I really such an idiot that I was ready to get on a boat with a stranger and have him take me, from what it sounds like, straight into the arms of a villain? I know villains. Kronos, for one. The Titans' leader is a shitty human being.

Although they haven't mentioned him, so I don't know what happened.

Cerberus, Wolfe James' dad, is another. He rules the Hell Hounds. Those two, him, and Kronos, are always at odds with each other.

So where does Ouranos fit in?

The silence catches my attention, and I suddenly tune back in to the conversation at hand. Well, the lack thereof. They're all staring at me, but Kade's eyebrows are up again.

I think I missed an important chunk of dialogue.

"What?" I ask, my voice gruff.

"You don't know who I am?" Kade asks.

Ah. "Well, no."

He stares at me. *Hard.* It does weird things to my chest, and it also somehow conjures back up the phantom sensation of his hand gripping the back of my neck.

"You were—"

"Ready to abscond with you off the island?" I take another sip of the coffee. I'm not convinced I *like* coffee, but my mouth is dry. "Yeah, dude. Anything to get away from her."

Artemis bristles.

I don't really mean it like that. I don't know why it came out that way.

"Typical Saint," Reese breathes. "Always talking out his ass."

I incline my chin.

Kade scoffs. He seems perplexed but also a bit angry.

"I didn't *choose* to have amnesia," I tell him.

"You did choose to be reckless." His gaze slides to Artemis. "And you decided to stay here to continue babysitting him?"

Continue?

I open my mouth, but Tem beats me to the punch.

"No, Kade." Her smile is positively brittle. Patronizing. "I've been here getting over the heroin addiction Gabriel forced on me."

The room goes quiet.

My gaze goes to her hand, the way her nails scratch at her arm over her long-sleeve shirt. Guilt trickles down my spine. I never once asked her why she was on the island with me—I just *assumed* it was to watch over me. Which, judging by a previous comment, is not unusual.

How long have I been with her?

And I don't mean *with*-with her—I still don't want to know how I knew her nipples were pierced. I mean, how long has she been stuck with my grumpy ass?

Reese straightens from where he'd been leaning a shoulder on the bookcase when Kade steps closer to Artemis. He's protective of her, it's clear to see. From pausing our fight in Lyssa's room, the way he holds Tem, watches her *and* watches out for her... he's there for her. He cares.

The flash of jealousy I feel is just a momentary setback.

I grit my teeth. There's a dull ache in the back of my head, a slow pulse that started so faintly, I didn't notice it until now.

But then Kade takes Tem's hand in his, and he carefully pushes her sleeve up her arm, past her elbow. He turns her palm up. There are small, dark bruises in the crook of her elbow.

When he coasts his thumb over them, she shudders.

She pulls out of his grasp and yanks her sleeve back into place.

"That's enough show and tell," she mutters. Her gaze moves around the room. "How much longer do we need to stay here?"

Kade doesn't reply. He just stares at her.

The mental image of his hulking, naked body coming out of the ocean floats in my vision, and I choke.

All the attention swings in my direction.

"You okay, buddy?" Reese asks.

My eyes are wide, and I point at Kade. "Is your dick pierced?"

15 REESE

WELL, this is awkward. Do I want to know how Saint knows—and I'm sure it's a *how* not an *if* because of Kade's wide smile—that his dick is pierced?

Artemis is turning a pretty shade of pink, too. She inches past Kade and comes straight to me, dropping her forehead to my chest. I put my hand on her hip, steadying her.

I feel bad for Saint. His face has gone tomato-red, too. I don't think he expected the question to come out, but it did. And now...

"Something to do with the ocean," Saint mutters.

Artemis says something, but her voice is too muffled by my shirt. She doesn't seem inclined to repeat it, though. It was probably an insult toward Saint.

I run my fingers through her hair at the nape of her neck, and she shivers.

Kade tilts his head. He shifts so we're all in his line of

sight. Years of knowing him helps me understand him better. He's a man of action and discipline—and yet, that seems to have all gone out the window in the past few years.

I mean, *Ouranos?* Really?

My fingers keep moving on Tem's skin, and she's slowly relaxing more against me.

"You can sit, you know," Kade says to me in a low voice. "You don't have to stand guard."

"I'm—"

His jaw tics.

Okay, fine.

I walk with Tem back to the couch and take a seat, and she twists to land on my lap, and she curls into me. Such a marked difference from the first time I saw her— when just my name made her faint.

Not gonna lie, being her safe person in this room swells pride in my chest.

"So. Back to the marina," Kade says. He sits across from Saint in the last remaining chair. They're all arranged to face the fireplace, which now houses a crackling fire behind a black metal grate. There's no television in here. Not much at all except the basics, and enough to make it cozy.

Cozy. In the winter. On an island.

But he wants to know about the marina explosion. Of course he would suspect me. He knows what we did overseas. My specialties.

I grimace, prepared not to say anything.

Tem lifts her head. "I'm curious, too."

"Okay, fine." I sigh. For her, it's easy to cave. "I saw Kade and Saint and suspected the worst."

She nods along, encouraging me.

"I went into a store and paid the cashier to call Kade. I just wanted him to keep him busy long enough for me to slip around and sabotage his boat. But when I got to the marina, I realized that sinking *his* wouldn't stop him. He'd just charter or steal one of the others to get back to Sterling Falls. Motivated bastard."

Kade scoffs.

"The harbormaster was asleep in his office. I stole his keys to get into the maintenance shed, and from there it was relatively easy to rig some stuff together." I make a face. "I made sure that everyone was out of range. The harbormaster was a bit pissed off at being woken up until I made something up about his car being towed. Then... well..."

"What?" Saint asks, leaning forward.

"It was bigger than I planned." I wince. "I'm rusty."

Tem bursts out laughing.

I still. "What?"

"You meant a *little* explosion?"

"Just some fire—"

Her giggles continue. "Fuck, Reese, I felt the ground shake outside of town."

Yeah. "I didn't realize the maintenance shed was also for the town. It had some fertilizer and other flammable stuff in. That's my best guess anyway."

That's putting it mildly.

Kade rolls his eyes. He pulls out his phone and scans

it, then quickly stashes it again. "Coast Guard is here. And Dr. Hawthorne has been blowing up my phone. Excuse the expression."

"She's calling because of Saint?" Tem bites her lip. "I sort of raised that alarm."

Kade nods once, his expression unreadable. "I need to return to town. You and Saint should show your faces to Dr. Hawthorne, as well."

My grip tightens on Tem's hip. "And, what, leave me here to take the fall?"

"When have I ever let you take the fall?" Kade snaps. "You *are* responsible, and I have no doubt you collected some witnesses along the way. So you can stay here while the three of us smooth things over with the proper people —me with the authorities, them with the psychiatrist."

"Gotta say, dude, I'm not really a fan of this."

Tem puts her palm on my cheek. "Thank you for keeping Saint safe. Now let's keep *you* safe. And we should get over there before dark." Her voice pitches to a whisper when she adds, "Besides, there are some things I imagine you need to discuss with Kade?"

Ah, yes. Of course.

Because what's the point of Isle of Paradise if we don't try to fix our issues?

16 KADE

"LYSSA LAURENT."

I freeze just inside the doorway.

Honestly, I thought I might get lucky and Reese would've fallen asleep while I was out. He was angry the last time I saw him, sitting on the bench by the beach. Angry at *me*. For decisions I've been making for my family.

My sister.

Whose name just came out of his mouth.

"Lyssa Laurent," he repeats. "She's a resident here on the island. The *other* residents call her Sleeping Beauty. Isn't that a clever nickname? She hasn't woken up in years, but the center is paid a very pretty penny to keep her body in good shape. Physical therapists and whoever else make sure her muscles don't atrophy too badly. The feeding tube. Regular grooming—although I would expect that for any comatose patient."

I'm across the room in a flash, my hand around his throat. I slam him into the wall, my rage brimming closer to the surface than ever before.

Only the fire behind the grate, which he must've kept alive, illuminates the space. The light and shadows flicker across his features.

"The secret of Kade Laurent lies with his comatose sister," Reese whispers. "Isn't that right?"

My grip tightens.

He doesn't even try to break it. He just stares at me, his green eyes boring into mine, and waits.

How the *fuck* did he find out about her?

When his eyes start to roll back, I loosen my hold. He sags back against the wall, and I stagger away, clutching at my head. I almost just killed him. I would've—*no, I would not have.* I could've, though. I could've just kept squeezing.

"You've kept her safe for years." Reese's voice is hoarse and scratchy. "After the horror that she went through in Terror."

I close my eyes.

"And she's exactly the reason why Gabriel wants to hurt Tem."

I whirl back to face him.

He rubs at his throat. "You found both of them, didn't you? But she was already gone."

"Two years ago, Gabriel had Lyssa transferred to Isle of Paradise. She spent time there as a kid, and I made sure I was her emergency contact back then. Her parents didn't give a shit—her issues were too much for them. It was easy for me to take over in that regard. When Gabriel brought her in, they called me. It was the first time I had any idea she was alive—and then the truth of her existence was revealed to me."

Reese waits for more.

"Gabriel was the real segue into my relationship with Ouranos," I admit. "He wanted me to stick close to him in Emerald Cove. It was... weird. He wasn't all there, in a way. But whenever he saw me, he talked about Lyssa. He wanted to know about her childhood. And then, one day, Ouranos came along."

A chill sweeps down my spine. Gabriel *never* mentioned Lyssa in front of him. The unassuming man stood like he had the power to destroy the world—and he would if someone tested him. He had no problem proving himself, be it through external leverage or mind games.

I was trying to find Reese at the time. Lyssa had slotted into place, but *Reese* had vanished. Ouranos offered me jobs that could fund my search, but it was never enough. I hit dead ends over and over. I dug myself deeper with Ouranos until I couldn't see a way out.

And when I had nothing left to give, he offered one final thing: physical evidence of Reese's location. The photo from the bank in Emerald Cove.

He said I could take that, and his resources, and find Reese.

In exchange, I sold my soul.

Gabriel didn't have such qualms. The promises Ouranos made him were between them—although, later,

I realized it was Artemis served up on a platter for him to twist and torture.

His revenge lives on, even now. His bloodlust hasn't been satiated.

"Does he visit her?" Reese eyes me. "Will the marina incident get back to him and raise suspicion?"

I lift my shoulder. "Probably."

"And Saint?"

"Ouranos took an interest because I took an interest." I look away. "Rather, he brought his interest to my attention because of that. He doesn't know my interest also extends to Artemis. He assumed my involvement with her was purely transactional."

"But it's not." He shoves himself up and steps toward me. "You hurt her—"

"Not planning on it."

The laugh that comes out of his mouth is chilly. "You already have. You actively betray her at every turn. It's *her* city."

"Sterling Falls is a fucked-up place." My tone is dismissive. "There's no saving it. Not from Ouranos. Not from the next bastard who comes along with aspirations of power."

Reese pivots and strides away from me. I trail him into the kitchen, my brows furrowed. He hits the light switch, and I almost wince at the brightness of the overhead bulbs. He goes straight to the freezer and pulls out a cold bottle of vodka.

Wordlessly, I retrieve two glasses. We should probably figure out food—there's some shelf-stable stuff in the pantry, and the water that comes out of the tap is clean and safe to drink—but I follow his lead and let him pour the liquor.

He drinks his.

I mirror him. It burns on the way down, in the way only vodka does. It pools like fire in my belly and slowly spreads.

"Take off your jacket," Reese mutters. "Stay awhile."

"You have any other clothes?"

"No."

I jerk my head toward the hallway that's barely visible from where we stand. "There's stuff in the bedroom if you want to change."

"You keep stuff here?"

"I wanted contingencies." I shift. "I bought this place as an abandoned cabin for a steal of a price. Every time I came out to visit Lyssa, I worked on it. Repaired the leaks in the roof, replaced the broken windows, redid the bathroom. Tiled the fucking shower and this backsplash." I gesture to the white and yellow tiles between the counter and upper cabinets.

"A real-life handyman."

"Shut up."

Reese pours more vodka into my glass. He lifts his. "Cheers, *brother*. To you and your contingencies."

WE'RE drunk by the time Saint and Artemis make their way back to us. I didn't fill Reese in on what the guy at the marina said. He took my statement and insurance information—the boat was a rental, so what the fuck do I really care—and said there would be ferries coming in as soon as the fire marshals deem it safe.

Saint and Artemis are better dressed for the weather, but it's clearly snowing. They stamp their shoes off and enter in matching bright-red coats. Saint removes his as fast as possible, like he's allergic to the fabric, and hangs it on one of the hooks by the door. Artemis does the same, but slower. Her shirt rides up in the back when she raises her arms, exposing a slice of muscled golden skin.

Too drunk to think things about the pretty little goddess.

I lean back on the couch, throwing my arm wide. It's that or stand and get myself in trouble lumbering up to her.

Or Saint.

Him asking about my cock was unexpected—and so was Tem's blush. We'll revisit that later, hopefully. When their inhibitions have lowered.

"You two have to catch up," I inform them.

I gesture to the empty glasses, the half-gone bottle between it. Reese has been heavy-lidded for an hour, his gaze on the fire. The conversation between us died out, and he only left briefly to raid my closet. He returned in black sweatpants and an orange hoodie.

Artemis makes a beeline for the bottle. She lifts it to her mouth and tips it back, her throat working as she takes one swallow, then another.

"Damn, girl," Reese breathes.

"You two just sitting here drinking?" Saint asks.

She sets the bottle down without offering it to him.

Someone was probably a dick to her this evening. I'd put money on that. Her hair is clean and braided, and snowflakes cling to it. She tugs the braid over her shoulder and toys with the end of it.

"That's how you and I became friends," Reese informs him. "Drinking and talking."

Saint freezes. "Really?"

"Yep. So take a seat. Maybe we'll make it fun and throw in a game."

Artemis perks up. "You got playing cards around here, Kade?"

I consider her and slowly nod. "Top drawer in the desk."

She spots it tucked under the back window. There's a lamp on it—off, for now—and a chair. I used to puzzle out ways of waking up Lyssa, or doing my finances, or sketching new renovation projects for this place when my money would flow.

Back then, I was hopeful Ouranos would pay me enough to allow that.

Now, I know he gave me just enough to keep me coming back for more.

"Aha!" She returns and takes a seat on the floor across from Reese and me.

We both landed on the couch earlier. Her back is to the fire, though, and it must be warm. She probably picked the smartest spot to sit. She taps out the deck from its box. She shuffles, the thrum of the cards against each other oddly soothing. While she does, Saint lowers himself to the floor beside her.

"Strip poker?" she suggests.

Saint chokes.

She elbows him. "Come on. You never got your answer about Kade's piercing."

17   ARTEMIS

I DIDN'T EXPECT the card shark to be Reese Avery. I glare at his three aces and two jacks. How does someone with such an innocent face harbor such *good* cards? If he wasn't shirtless—the shirt and his hoodie are the only items of clothing he's lost so far—I'd accuse him of hiding cards up his sleeves.

We took a while to come to an agreement on the rules. The one with the best hand can either choose to put back *on* a piece of clothing, or everyone who didn't fold removes an item. Socks count individually.

I'm a little fuzzy around the edges of my thoughts because I've been drinking. I'm pretty sure that's against the rules. Is getting drunk going to mess with my recovery? But also... I'd be going crazy if I had to survive this night sober. It's bad enough that the craving for heroin has once more reared its ugly head. It occupies every other thought.

The only thing saving me is that no one has the drug here. I can't beg or plead with Kade or Reese or, fuck, even Saint, to give me the syringe. I can't slip out and go hunt down a drug dealer, because I'm pretty sure all three of them would murder me.

Reese and Kade from disappointment, and Saint just to get away from me.

"Well?" I grit out at Reese.

Saint folded early. He's been sucking, though, and is down to one sock and his boxers.

Kade still has his jeans and shirt on, and most likely boxers or briefs underneath, but his sweatshirt and both socks are gone.

And me? Oh, I'm preserving my sanity the best I can in my sports bra and panties.

If I win, I'm one hundred percent putting on a sweatshirt. The fire roaring behind us has heated up the cabin, but I'm still chilled.

Reese smirks. "Lose an item, golden girl."

I narrow my eyes.

Kade coughs, but he doesn't seem to care about *his* situation. I mean, he lost with a freaking pair of sevens. Who stays in with a pair of *sevens*? He's still got a shirt to lose, too.

He rises, nonchalant, and unbuttons his jeans. When he lowers them, I gasp. He didn't go for the obvious clothing choice—but worse: he's not wearing boxers *or* briefs.

The thick appendage that hangs between his legs is

suddenly out, loud and proud. And, *you're welcome, Saint*, pierced.

Reese laughs. "Damn, dude."

Kade rolls his eyes and sits back down, but his gaze lingers on Saint. His shirt is loose enough to sort of cover him. I just need to stop staring between his legs. And stop staring in general. Or looking. Definitely should not be looking.

Kade Laurent is trouble. I've said that since day one.

I shrug out of my sports bra. I set it down beside me and resist the urge to cover my breasts. My nipples pebble, reacting to the cold.

We deal another hand.

"Want to make it more interesting, Hart?" Kade asks.

Saint lifts his shoulder. "What do you have in mind?"

"You lose to *me*, you lose two items of clothing. No folding."

I gotta admit, seeing Saint's tattooed cock next to Kade's pierced one would be a mental image I'd like to hold on to forever. And use it for my spank bank until I die. My gaze bounces between them like I'm watching a tennis match. Saint considers his cards, then Kade's face, and finally nods.

He leans forward, stretching his arm across the table, and shakes Kade's hand.

My cards suck. I toss them in, unwilling to part with my panties.

Saint trades in three cards.

Reese winks at me and asks for one.

Kade takes none.

"Oh, you're fucked," I whisper to Saint.

"Shut up."

Saint reveals a straight with a slow smile. The bastard actually got lucky, which seems like a miracle after he took *three* cards.

Reese drops his cards on the table. I inch forward and take in his five clubs.

A flush is better than Saint's straight...

"Let's see it, Laurent," Saint says.

Kade puts his cards down, and I immediately laugh.

Of fucking course.

He has a straight flush. The spades seem to laugh up at us, and I focus on Saint.

"You can lose an item, too," Kade says to Reese.

Reese shrugs and pulls off a sock. He drops it to the cushion beside him and points to Saint. "I think that means you have to get naked."

"I don't like this game," Saint mutters.

Still, he's not a whiny bitch about it. He yanks his sock off and throws it at Kade, then shimmies out of his boxers. The sight of his tattooed dick flips my stomach, and I fight against the wave of memories of feeling it inside me.

The arousal burns between my legs, and I shift my weight to press my thighs together.

"How about a new game?" Reese asks. "Since you guys have both lost this one."

I snort. "Like?"

"Truth or dare?"

"A children's game, then," Saint says.

Reese just smiles.

"Fine." I tilt my head at Reese. "Lose your jeans and put us on even footing."

"Is that a dare?"

"Yeah, it is."

His smile widens. He rises and removes his sweatpants, then briefs. They're not the ones he was wearing last night—he's not in *any* of the same clothing. And they don't exactly fit perfectly, which makes me think Kade supplied him with stuff.

How nice of him.

"My turn," Reese announces. "Saint. Truth or dare?"

"Truth."

"Have you remembered anything else and not told?" Reese asks.

Saint wets his lips. "Just confusing stuff. I don't know what's real or not."

"Like?" Reese prods.

"A kiss."

I make a noise in the back of my throat, but he's not looking at me.

He meets Kade's steady gaze.

Oh, fuck. Oh my God. Why is the idea of that such a turn-on? It shouldn't be, right? But Saint's heart has been flayed open time and again, and he struggled with letting me in. Maybe it's not just me who's needed to fix him.

Maybe he needs more.

I can't always be the martyr of this relationship. I can't always sacrifice myself over and over hoping that it'll fix Saint. The thought hits me like a thunderclap, and

I dig my nails into my thighs. The bit of pain comes through my tipsy haze, and it allows me to hold on to that thought more solidly.

Saint might need more than just me. Even if he fell in love with me on his own... I'm just one person.

The thought scares me a little, because the flip side of the coin is that this is *Kade* we're talking about. I don't trust him. Like Reese said, he's not going to kill us. That doesn't account for him giving me to Gabriel, and he clearly has no morals when it comes to Sterling Falls. Does he have morals when it comes to Saint?

Or me now?

"My turn," Saint continues, oblivious to my line of thinking. "Kade? Truth or dare."

"Dare." Kade's smile is positively wicked.

"If my memory is real..." He grimaces. "Don't fuck with me. Just prove it."

Kade nods once. He stands and motions for Saint to do the same.

I scramble to my feet and get out of the way, finding Reese's side on the couch. He automatically loops his arm around my shoulders.

Saint seems paralyzed. He faces Kade, but some sort of flight response triggers when he gets close. Saint steps away, and Kade follows. Slowly, like a dance, until Saint's back hits the far wall. He straightens up off it, his brows furrowing.

With a sudden move, Kade shoves Saint back.

I gasp, but Reese's hand leaves my shoulder and covers my mouth.

Yeah, right. This is important memory time, here.

Still, the thought of this happening at some point, and Saint not *mentioning* it? The *when* will be my next question. If I get a next question.

Saint pushes at Kade's hands, but he shoves harder. He grasps Saint's hips, pinning him to the wall, and looks down between them.

"Hmm," Kade murmurs. "Same bodily response."

Reese brushes my arm with his knuckles. The feeling trails down, to my hip, then inches under my panties.

Fuck.

Saint doesn't resist it. His eyes are wide when Kade leans in, and Kade places the tiniest, softest of kisses on Saint's lips.

Once.

Twice.

Reese's fingers dip inside me, and his other hand holds my jaw closed. The groan that wants to come out is trapped behind my teeth.

When Kade pulls away, Saint follows.

Kade grips Saint's jaw, catching his motion, and tips his head. He kisses him deeper, their mouths opening. Tongues sliding.

Hot.

Hot, hot, hot.

Reese teases my clit, his fingers featherlight, until I squirm against him. I can't look away, but I would bet money that he's hard, too. I tear my gaze off Saint and Kade and twist, throwing my leg over Reese's lap.

Let them have their moment—I want to chase this one.

Reese immediately leans in and kisses my collarbone. I roll my hips forward, grinding on his erect cock. His knuckles bump me as he fists it, pumping slowly, and when I rise, he runs the tip of it down my center.

I lower, taking him inside me, and exhale shakily. His lips trail to my throat, and my eyes close. His hands are *everywhere*. On my hips, palming my breasts—

Another hand drifts between my legs, and my breath stutters. I open my eyes and glance over my shoulder, meeting Kade's gaze. It's his hand between my legs, his other on my breast. He pulls at the bar in my nipple, sending tingling pleasure straight through my chest.

He presses on my clit. Pinches it.

"Oh," I gasp.

Reese takes my chin and redirects my face back toward his. He kisses me hard, his hips rolling to thrust himself deeper inside me. Poor Reese—I hadn't moved. I lift now, lowering myself. He slides into me easily.

While Kade plays with my clit and my nipple, Reese's hands move elsewhere. From my throat down the center of my chest, to my hips. Back up, tangling in my braid.

Too soon, the pleasure builds into an unstoppable force. Kade's patience, Reese's slow strokes—it's too much. I gasp into Reese's mouth, my back arching. Even with closed eyes, I see white for a long moment.

"Worth the wait." Kade's lips brush my ear. His

breath is warm. He steps back, and cooler air touches my spine.

I hadn't realized he was so close.

But—*Saint.* I whip my head around and find Saint leaning against the wall, exactly where Kade left him. His eyes are wide, his lips swollen. His cock stands straight out, and he seems just as shocked as me.

Reese nips my neck. "The vodka has stolen my ability to fuck you properly, golden girl." He pats my ass.

Carefully, I lift off him. His cock, too, is an angry red. It's wet from my arousal, but he ignores it to help me to my feet.

"Artemis will take my room," Kade says. He's already dragging his jeans back into place. "Saint and Reese, double up in the spare room. I'll take the couch."

That seems to kick everyone into motion. Everyone except me anyway. My mind seems to have fractured from the climax—brought on with an astounding assist by Kade.

Saint comes over and grabs his clothes, turning away to get dressed. Reese seems less concerned, although he follows Saint down the hall, and I'm left with Kade.

He holds out his sweatshirt.

I debate for a second, then take it from him. The warm, heavy fabric swamps me, and I sneak a deep inhale before my head pops out. The hem hits me mid-thigh. My panties are still in place—funny how that happened. How *all* that happened with the center strip shifted a bit to the side...

"This doesn't change anything," I finally say. "I still don't trust you."

"Good." He shakes his head. "I have lies built on ulterior motives, Tem. You shouldn't trust me."

A chill sweeps through me.

I point to his shirt. "You did all of that without taking it off."

"Yeah."

"You took off your jeans, knowing you weren't wearing underwear, before your shirt."

His chin rises.

It hits me—*the tattoo*. I choke on my laugh. The tattoo on his chest, in a very similar position to mine, was done by the one and only Saint Hart. That would be a clear indication to Saint about their relationship.

"He's going to see it eventually."

His dark eyes bore into mine. "How did he react when he saw yours?"

I suck my lower lip between my teeth. "Well, I was hypothermic from him shoving me into the ocean. So I don't think we even talked about it."

His eyebrows hike. "Excuse me?"

"Saint and I do not get along." I pick at my nails. I feel a little more naked than usual right this very second, admitting that to him. "It was a long year before you and Reese came around."

He doesn't say anything for so long, I figure that's the end of it. I shake my head and turn to go to bed. My thoughts are still fuzzy around the edges. Just enough to guarantee nightmares.

"You'll get him back."

My shoulders inch higher.

Behind me, Kade sighs. "You will, Tem. He'll come back to you."

I roll out the tension and glance back. "Didn't know you were an optimist, Kade. In Sterling Falls—and Isle of Paradise—that's foolish-adjacent."

Almost as foolish as hoping Lyssa will wake up.

18 ARTEMIS

DR. HAWTHORNE MEETS me in the trees. She hands me a mug from the cafeteria. Her long, beige coat is buttoned up to her throat, the collar upturned against the cold wind.

It's early. Too early for me to be out of bed—and *much* too early for trekking around the island. We have a view of the water from here, and up ahead, around the corner, is their dock. It has a boat tied off there, manned by a guy with a gun.

"You snuck out?" The doc's tone is mild.

"I did warn you."

She sighs. "I was hoping you were joking."

Nope.

She hid her annoyance yesterday well. The concern overrode it, and she brought Saint and I into her office to interrogate us. She was worried about Kade, of course, but Saint did his part and lied about him. I took the fall for a bad assumption, explaining that my trauma must've muddled my perception.

It was a load of shit, but it worked out okay.

And *then,* after she dismissed Saint, I explained that we had some friends on the island and needed to spend some time with them. For our health.

I mean, I guess I didn't exactly tell her we were going to sneak out after bed check, but close enough. She could've locked me in my room, but she didn't.

So... it's on her.

Technically speaking.

"Did you have a good visit?"

I scan the water. "We're trapped, in a way, right?"

"Trapped?"

"We can't leave." I take a sip of the coffee. It's good— maybe a little too much creamer, but tasty nonetheless. "That's the definition of trapped."

"Trapped implies..."

"Claustrophobia?"

She nods. "Or?"

"Like an animal in one of those metal claws. Some will gnaw off their own leg to escape."

Her attention shifts more directly onto me. "Do you feel the need to gnaw off your own leg to escape?"

"Not currently."

We're facing Sterling Falls, but it's out of sight. Too far across the water. It's only sometimes visible on a clear night.

"But...?"

"But perhaps some other residents might get restless.

If they know they can't actually leave." I shrug. "Just a thought."

"Do you have someone in particular you're worried about?"

I debate. "Perhaps I should check on Lyssa Laurent."

"Perhaps."

"She squeezed my hand. She could open her eyes at any moment."

"You mentioned that," she murmurs.

"I really think she could wake up."

"Hope is a good thing to hold on to in dark times, Artemis. But it can also be dangerous."

"I told Kade that optimism was adjacent to foolishness."

"How do you feel about that?"

"I think I hit the nail on the head." I pause. "But perhaps being foolish isn't the worst trait in the world right now. Burying my head in the sand would be easier."

"Hmm." She tips her head toward the buildings.

We slowly make our way in that direction. My mug is empty by the time we get to the door, and she takes it back from me. Inside, I'd go right to get to Lyssa's room, and she'd go left to return the mug—or left and then up the stairs to reach her office.

"I don't consider you a fool," she finally says. "And I know you'll do what's right to protect those who can't protect themselves."

Goosebumps erupt down the backs of my arms. She walks away without a backward glance. That sounded like she knows... *more*. More than anything I told her about my past.

Weird.

It's weird, right?

I reach Lyssa's room, but the door is open. There are voices coming from inside. I pause, straining to hear. Dr. Hawthorne didn't say I *shouldn't* visit. And Kade was passed out on the couch when I left.

Besides, the voices are female.

Physical therapy?

Fuck it.

I step inside like I'm meant to be there, then stop dead. There's a doctor sitting on the edge of Lyssa's bed, and she seems to be holding one side of a conversation.

The girl formerly known as Sleeping Beauty is holding the other.

At my entrance, Lyssa turns to look at me. Her hazel eyes meet mine, and she offers a slow, inching smile. "Artemis."

I'm not proud of this—but between the vodka from last night, which may or may not still be in my blood, and now *this?*

I pass out.

SOMETHING COOL TOUCHES MY FOREHEAD. "She's coming around."

"...bumped her head."

"Probably should've foreseen..."

It seems to take forever for my hearing to even out. I blink up at the ceiling and the orderly hovering around me.

"Welcome back," he says.

I make a face and push up on my forearms.

"Easy does it." He grasps my shoulder.

"I'm good." I sit up, touching the back of my head. "That was embarrassing."

No one stops me from getting to my feet. I focus on Lyssa, half expecting her to be asleep like every other time. But *nope*, she's fucking awake. Sitting in a reclined bed position, pillows stacked behind her. Her body is probably weak, but her gaze is sharp enough to cut.

"Can we have a minute?" Lyssa asks.

The doctor and orderly both eye me. The orderly drags out a chair and motions for me to sit, then says something about getting juice for low blood sugar.

I take a seat and lean back in it. My skin is clammy, and I rub my palms down my thighs.

"Doc was just filling me in on..." She motions around the room. Her fingers are curled in, and the movement is jerky. She doesn't lift most of her arm. "The time wasted."

"A decade."

She sighs. "This room is..."

I try to see it for the first time. From her perspective. The last time she was conscious, she was trapped in Terror.

And now we're all trapped on this island.

"Excessive," she lands on. "They said I was back on Isle of Paradise."

Her gaze drifts to the window.

She seems a lot more poised than I would've thought. My head throbs, and I shift to rest my chin on my hand. Elbow on the arm of the chair.

Gabriel was always obsessed with Lyssa having a room with a view.

"So. How do you feel?"

She laughs under her breath. "Honestly? I'm tired."

Kade is going to freak the fuck out.

"Talking is exhausting. My eyes open..."

That's my cue, then. I push out of the chair and smile at her. The conflicting emotions inside me are too much. I'm happy for her. That she's awake. Completely confused about why she opened her eyes now—and what kept her unconscious for so long.

"I'll let you get some rest before your doctors come back." I put the chair between us, walking backward. If I look away, she might disappear.

Imagine.

"Artemis?"

I cock my head.

She shivers. Her head is already back against the pillow more, her body seeming to sink into the bed. "Never mind. Later."

Later.

"Promise?"

She barely manages a nod. I point, silently holding

her to it, and exit the room before I completely lose my mind and burst into tears.

I FOLLOW REESE TO TOWN. I'm in borrowed jeans, a thick, lined canvas jacket, and boots that are a size too big. He said we needed groceries, then paused and asked if I wanted to come along. Since I couldn't exactly go marching through the store in what is *clearly* trauma center uniform, we raided Kade's closet.

Part of me expected chatter. A never-ending stream of conversation from Reese. But, so far, he's remained stoically quiet.

It's more unsettling than I'd like.

He walks with a purpose. Shoulders back, strides long. Even though I'm fairly confident he doesn't know the exact way, or the best path, anyone who saw him would assume he does.

Before the whole *amnesia* thing, I walked like that. I knew my place in the world. I was next to Elora, of course. We were building a life together. Fighting at

Olympus, my tattoo shop, making masks... I knew what I wanted from life, and it was simple.

Maybe it wasn't *easy*, but I never wanted the big things. I didn't need huge, expensive vacations, or an extravagant house, or anything other than Elora.

I pull Kade's jacket tighter around me. It's loose in the shoulders, and the citrus scent keeps assaulting my nose every time I shift it.

That kiss is another thing entirely.

Expected? After the games we ended up playing?

Or... after the memory of it? I linger on *that*, now convinced my brain wasn't just spinning creative stories. He was more aggressive the first time. We were clothed, but he pinned me with his hips, his chest pressed to mine. His grip on my jaw was the same. The kisses were the same.

And then, we broke apart and stared at each other, and my fucking dick was standing straight up. He glanced from my eyes down to it, then over his shoulder. When he left me against the wall and went to Artemis and Reese, who were equally lost in their own world on the couch, my stomach twisted.

Because him touching her while Reese fucked her was probably much hotter than anything I could've conjured in my brain.

"We're guests of Kade's," Reese says over his shoulder.

It jars me away from the image of him and Artemis.

"If anyone asks. We came in with him the other day."

"Fine," I agree. "Better than telling people I've escaped from the insane asylum."

The people haven't been *all* that bad—and they're definitely not the old-school definition of insane. Misguided, maybe. Mistreated. Healing from trauma.

"Are you sure you should be going into town?" I catch up to him. "You know, since you're apparently a wanted felon?"

Reese scoffs. "I'm not. You, on the other hand..."

I rear back. "What?"

"You're an escapee from the trauma center. A pair of jeans won't hide that unless you act cool." He taps the brim of the cap he dug out of Kade's closet. "A hat does a lot in subterfuge. I'd know."

"Wouldn't you rather a pair of glasses, Clark Kent?"

A laugh bursts out of him. "Okay, good to know your pop culture knowledge is alive and well. What else is still rattling around in that brain of yours?"

I lift one shoulder. That's the very question I've been asking myself. But then I focus on the last thing he said—about knowing about subterfuge. "How would you know?"

"Military."

I tilt my head.

"It's where I met Kade, you know. Confusing bastard. He can be so noble—" Reese presses his lips together, seeming to stop his words from coming out. "I learned a lot working with him, but we each had our specialties."

"What was his?" Curiosity tugs at me.

Reese smirks. "Giving orders. I think you know that one a little. Or, you will soon enough."

"I'm not—" It's my turn to swallow my words. I'm not *what*? Bisexual? I have no idea what the fuck I am anymore. I don't know what happened in the last two years. Maybe something twisted inside me, or maybe it was always there. Or *maybe* it's just Kade's energy.

"Do you want to remember?" he asks.

I'm saved from replying, because the buildings of the small town suddenly come into view. The truth is, I don't know if I want to remember. I don't know if where I am now is any better than where I was.

20 ARTEMIS

THERE'S a note on the counter. Reese and Saint went to get supplies. And Kade... I search the cabin for him, only to find him outside. He's chopping wood, his tight black shirt doing absolutely nothing to hide his bunching muscles.

Kade unfortunately has the sort of muscular back that makes my mouth water.

Add that in with memories of what happened last night...

I swallow my desire and focus on the facts. Like, that Kade's a traitor, he nearly stole Saint yesterday, *and* he opened the door for Ouranos to take over Sterling Falls. He was responsible for a lot of my heartache, even if his strings were being pulled from afar.

"I can feel you watching me." Kade's voice jars my thoughts just as he swings the axe down. The wood splits with a satisfying *crack*, the two halves falling off the stump.

"It's better to keep my eye on you than leave you unsupervised."

He buries the tip of the axe in the stump and turns to face me. His skin glistens with sweat. "Is that why you snuck out at the crack of dawn?"

I wave my hand, dismissing that. For some reason, I'm not exactly ready to admit that Lyssa is awake. He'd probably go rushing to her side, getting all distracted from the matter at hand...

"Why is it you always show up when things are at their worst?" I blurt out.

"Maybe I have remarkably bad timing." He crosses to the porch and snags his shirt from the rail. Instead of putting it on, he uses the fabric to wipe at his face and chest.

"Bad timing doesn't sell out your—" *Jesus*, I was about to call him a friend. Saint and I went to *him* for help when Reese was taken by Gabriel. "I trusted you. But you lied to us, you sabotaged us—"

"I was trying to protect you, Tem."

"No. No, you weren't."

His gaze softens. "Gabriel never would've released his hold on Reese. But after—*after*, Tem, when Ouranos arrived, that's when I did what I could to get you all out."

"Which means you were only protecting yourself in the end." I cross my arms over my stomach. It rolls on the coffee I drank earlier, the shakiness of my fainting coming roaring back. My skin is clammy. "You put just enough care into your actions to make it hurt worse."

He freezes. No doubt remembering that so-called

care he used to pull me from the tub, brush my hair, dress me. And countless other little actions, even when he wasn't supposed to be anywhere near us.

"Would it be better if I didn't care at all?"

I lift my chin. "It would be better if you stayed away from us."

His gaze is incredulous. "You think I don't know that? You think I don't replay every second of what I did and wish I could rewrite it? Fuck that, Artemis. I have nightmares about how my actions led to *this*." He motions at me.

All this, and he's still on their fucking side. The side that wants to destroy and take over my city. The insidious, invading, murdering side.

"Then why are you still playing the villain?" I shout. "Why cling to the role like it makes any of this noble?"

"Because it's easier than hoping for forgiveness I'll never deserve." His voice is hollow.

Hope is destructive.

Hope is dangerous.

I know that, just as well as anyone else. But would I chose evil over *hope*?

"That's the difference between us, Kade," I say quietly. "I'd never sell someone out just to make myself feel better."

He looks away, his cheeks pinkening. "Yeah. I know."

I sigh. This is not how I wanted the conversation to go. He turns away, back to the job at hand, but stops when I call his name.

"By the way, your sister is awake."

I WAS RIGHT—KADE bolted for Lyssa as soon as the words registered. I, by contrast, actually get a moment to breathe and enjoy the empty cabin. How long has it been since I've been *alone*? Like, truly? Stolen nights in my apartment at Bow & Arrow don't necessarily count.

I take a hot shower, and even the gross two-in-one shampoo and conditioner can't dampen how good the water feels.

Dressed in oversized clothes that smell distinctly like Kade's citrus scent, I finger-comb my hair and wrap it in a towel, then go back to his room and flop on the bed.

Considering Kade...

He clearly cares about his sister. He bought this cabin to be near her, even though she was unconscious for a decade. He fixed it up enough to be a decent place to stay.

And his loyalty to Reese is undeniable.

I screw my eyes shut tighter, not liking that train of thought. Can I *blame* him for saving Reese? Not really. I would've given Kade up to save Saint, and I don't even particularly like Saint.

That's a lie.

I really, really, *really* don't like Saint.

For some reason, that thought brings a smile to my lips.

And in the next second, I'm crying.

Because *fuck Saint Hart.* Fuck his stupid memory

loss, and blaming me for being the bearer of bad news, and—

The front door creaks upon opening, and I sit up sharply. I dash the tears from my face and pull the towel from my head. My wet hair tumbles over my shoulders. Hopefully all the telltale signs of crying—red face, bloodshot and puffy eyes—will be overlooked.

Then again, I only cried for thirty seconds before getting interrupted.

Shaking it off, I exit the room and find Reese and Saint in the kitchen, unloading bags on the counter.

Saint glances up first, and the corner of his lips curl up. The almost-smile is immediately replaced by a scowl, and I roll my eyes. Trust him to be so pigheaded it hurts.

Reese, however, leaves what he's doing and envelops me in a hug. I let him fold me into his chest, the chill of winter still clinging to his jacket. I tip my head back, and he gives me exactly what I want: a kiss.

A soft peck. Nothing that should fire me up, but it does. The urge to jump his bones hits me hard, and I clutch harder at his jacket.

Calm down, Tem. Now's not the time. I separate myself from him, retreating to the far side of the kitchen. I rest my hip on the counter and cross my arms.

"Lyssa is awake," I inform them both.

Saint's scowl lifts into a shocked expression.

Reese's brows furrow. "How?"

I shrug. "Absolutely no idea. I doubt the doctors do either."

But I knew I wasn't imagining that hand

squeeze. Reflex or not... She's awake. Ten years later. If I thought Saint's memory issues were bad, I can't imagine waking up to a completely unfamiliar world.

The technology advances alone would be enough to make my head spin.

"That's where Kade went. To go see her."

Reese nods. "Now's our shot, then."

I tilt my head. "For what?"

"To leave him and get the fuck out of here." He exits the kitchen, returning with a duffel bag. Instead of putting groceries away, he shoves stuff into the bag.

I inch closer, spotting toiletries as he tucks them away. I lay my hand on his arm. "We can't go."

"What?"

"I—"

"Your brother is back in Sterling Falls, Tem," Reese says softly.

Saint perks. "Apollo? Was he traveling?"

I pinch the bridge of my nose.

"He and his family went to Emerald Cove. Gabriel—"

"Kade's accomplice," I interject.

Reese grimaces. "Gabriel cut them off from returning."

Saint seems confused. "Apollo has a family?"

Oh, for fuck's sake.

"He, Wolfe, and Jace are in a happy relationship with a woman named Kora."

"All three of them?"

"Well, Wolfe and Apollo have a bit of a relationship on their own, too…"

Saint's face flushes, and his eyes widen. "When—?"

"Sometime in the last two years." I make a face. "I keep forgetting you're missing the extraneous details, too. The relationship isn't my point. If my brother is back in Sterling Falls, that's all the more reason for us to just wait it out."

"You're scared." That comes from Saint. And, to no one's surprise, he has *asshole* in his tone.

"I'm not *scared*. I don't get scared." I glare at him. "I am cautious. *And*, I know my brother's family's strengths. They're more equipped to get Ouranos out of our town, and we can just come back when the coast is clear. They've done this before, after all."

They're practically experts at cleaning up the city. Yes, the last time a war broke out, it was gruesome and bloody, and we lost Nyx along the way…

"You're not the slightest bit curious—or concerned—about what's happening over there?" Reese asks me. "Antonio talked a lot about *before*. How you were the glue holding those guys together during the worst of it."

My throat closes.

"Antonio?"

"He and Vittoria have been staying at Kora's house with me." Reese comes up and cups my cheek. "And Daniel stayed, too."

"I know Daniel," Saint murmurs. "Tech guy. He was never around much, though."

"Tech guy," I agree. "Came in clutch last year."

Reese drags his palm over his face, hiding a smile. "He took over the dining room table with all his computers and hard drives and wires. He was driving Vittoria crazy. Probably still is."

My smile is weak.

How can I deny going back when all the people I care about are there and waiting for me?

But... maybe Saint is partially right. Underlying my bravado isn't fear—it's craving. Sterling Falls is a gateway back to the drugs that have finally left my system. When I think about going back, my mind turns to Gabriel and his chaos, but also the rush that came with hitting the plunger and injecting the heroin into my bloodstream.

And it's the craving that terrifies me.

"I'm surprised you want to ditch Kade," Saint says to Reese.

"Your view of him is probably colored by your dick," Reese replies.

I snort.

"You could give him a chance," Saint mutters.

After a long moment, Reese blows out a breath. "Okay, fine. I'll give him a chance—but don't forget that he's working for the enemy. He shouldn't be trusted."

On that, we agree.

21 GABRIEL

SOMETHING IS WRONG.

I scan the horizon. It seems normal out here, which is to say *quiet*. Peaceful, even. It's the sort of view I always craved. Wide-open spaces.

And yet, it's those same spaces that make my skin crawl.

Something has always been wrong with me. I'm more comfortable in the dark or by myself. I oscillate between wanting silence and *noise*. So much deafening noise, I feel it vibrate in my chest.

That's why explosions are so nice. It's both combined. Nothing, then *everything*.

The body under me jerks. I rise a little, bringing my knee off the small of his back, and drag his head out of the water by his hair. His face hovers over the surface, still, until I thump his back.

He coughs, water pouring out of his nose and mouth. His body flinches, spasming.

Such a big man, I thought he would at least give me a challenge. But all it took was a few pokes, and down fell the giant. The hardest part was dragging his body into the ocean.

"I hate sand," I tell him. "It gets *everywhere*. I'll be finding it weeks later in my shoes or a crease in my shirt. It's nature's glitter."

He pushes at me, his fingers slick with water.

Oh, and blood.

Lots of blood.

Where we are, the water surges and recedes, but we don't get his with those pesky white-capped waves. We're still practically on the shore.

It leaves us, and he's now looking at wet sand.

There *was* a face impression in it earlier.

His face.

Now, there's only some bumps and ridges remaining.

I release him, and he barely catches himself on his forearms. A face-plant would've been a good laugh. I rock back on my heels, considering him.

Blood leaks from his stomach, staining his wet gray shirt. Nasty wound.

"I wonder if I punctured your intestines," I muse. "Then I wouldn't have to drown you. I could wait for your body to poison itself."

He focuses on me and misses the rushing wave. It slams into his face, submerging him. He raises himself higher, but these waves just keep coming. He'd have to sit up to clear it.

I don't think his legs work anymore, though. I made a

few slices. Cutting through muscle is surprisingly easy if you have a sharp enough blade.

He struggles to raise his face and fails. Instead, smart man that he is, he heaves himself over onto his back. The water now works with him, his face angled to the sky, even as another wave rolls over and makes him sputter. Still, he gets the reprieve.

"He *does* have brains," I whisper to myself.

When the water rushes back once again, he's left flat on his back in the sand, staring up at the starless night, dazed.

The *wrongness* prickles at me again.

"Here's what's going to happen." I fist my hand in his shirt just under his chin. "Next wave is coming, so you've got about thirty seconds. Do I hold you under or lift you up and you tell me what I want to know?"

He gapes at me. There's saltwater and blood on his lips. A blood vessel burst in his eye, giving his stare a ghoulish feel.

"Oh, right. You don't know what I want to know." My gaze rises. "Oops, too late."

The water pours over him. His arms flail, knocking into my legs, but I am less moveable than a boulder. My muscles tense, holding him under. In less than a minute, he'll be able to breathe again. He just needs to not fight it.

Artemis didn't fight me on it. Of course, it wasn't the rush of *water* that dragged her under—it was heroin. She let it sweep her far, far away.

The man chokes and coughs when he can take in a lungful of air.

"Right, now, what I wanted to know..." I lean in. "Tell me about the Hell Hounds."

His face contorts.

Fury.

I tsk. "Did you not think *that* was what I wanted? Did you think I was going to ask you about Olympus, perhaps? That's where I found you creeping like a spider through the shadows..."

He gurgles out a sound. A word.

"Try again." My patience runs thin. "Clearer. *Enunciate.* You're trying to save your own life, aren't you?"

He wets his lips. His gaze bores into mine, and he manages two clear-as-day words. They're just not the ones I want to hear.

"*Fuck off.*"

I unfold my knife. His gaze goes to the gleaming tip, and he tries to push me off or away. It's no matter. I've broken most of his body, and now comes the rest of it. I drop his shirt and straddle him, batting at his hands. I sit hard on the wound on his stomach. A deep grunt releases from his chest, more pain than he thought possible.

"This was my own fault," I say sadly. I carefully slide the blade between his ribs. "You took such a full, deep breath. A *lungful.* It made me think what would happen if your lungs just couldn't hold air anymore."

He feels it right away. The puncture. A pneumothorax, as they call it.

"*Please,*" he wheezes.

"Please, what? Please save your life? Please let you die? Please, feed your cat? Tell your loved ones you're so fucking sorry for leading the life of a motorcycle gangster with who knows *how* many deaths on your hands?" I rise and step off him. "No. No to all of that. You didn't help me, so I cannot help you."

I wait for the next wave to come and rinse his blood from my hands.

Metaphorically and literally.

Leaving him where he is, I dust the stupid sand from my soaked jeans and head back to my motorcycle.

A Cyclops awaits me. He seems vaguely green in the face—or maybe that's just the garish yellow streetlight overhead. It's messing with my color perception.

"Boss wants to see you." His gaze moves past me to the man. "Is that guy dead?"

I make a face. "Does he look dead to you?"

"I—"

"He's not. Not yet anyway." I glance over my shoulder. "I suppose he might be useful. Go and fetch him before he fades away."

The Cyclops moves to follow my order, then pauses. "Who is he?"

I smile. "The leader of the Hell Hounds."

22   KADE

LYSSA IS ASLEEP.

The good kind, luckily. It's actually much noisier than her comatose form. Her chest rises and falls less evenly, her lips are parted, and she occasionally shifts and twitches.

We had a chat before her eyes got heavy. I held her hand. Maybe I cried a little—sue me.

Dr. Hawthorne comes in and takes stock of the room, then tips her head toward the door.

I let Lyssa's hand slide from mine and follow her into the hall.

"How are you holding up, Mr. Laurent?" she asks, her voice and expression full of concern.

I shake my head. "I don't know. Trying to wrap my head around reality."

She nods in understanding. "Lyssa has a long road ahead of her. Physical therapy, in tandem with talk therapy... she's awake, but her journey has only gotten more complex."

"Right."

"She needs to build up her muscles and learn how to use her body again. It's a great sign that she is talking and seems cognizant of where she is."

"Because she used to live here."

Dr. Hawthorne pauses. "Yes, well, from my understanding there was quite a bit of trauma between that stay and the start of this one."

"Yes." I clear my throat. "I want what's best for her. If we need to fly in a specialist—do it. Whatever it takes."

"Don't expect overnight miracles, Mr. Laurent."

"I'm not."

She smiles. "Should I expect you to stick around for a while, then? The moral support will be a huge factor. And continued support throughout her treatment. Of course, I don't expect you to be here every day. Checking in on her, however... I know you're good for that."

"I'll be here until work tears me away."

My voice is steady, but *work* is just a euphemism for *Ouranos.* He allowed me the time off to check on my sister, but I'm almost certain he did not expect me to still be here. My phone was left in the boat, which means it's currently at the bottom of the harbor.

Fuck. He's probably tried to call—and I didn't even consider that until right this moment. Talk about being distracted. By three troublemakers: Saint and Artemis and Reese.

"Speaking of work, I need to check in, and my phone isn't working. Can I borrow yours?"

Dr. Hawthorne leads me to her office and gestures to the landline at her desk. "Dial nine first to get an outside line."

She leaves me alone, and I sit at her desk. Was it really only yesterday that I was sitting in this office considering breaking into the filing cabinet? And then Saint walked in...

I shake my head and dial the number I was forced to memorize.

It rings twice, then Ouranos' cold voice answers, "Not many people have this private number."

"Luckily, you gave it to me," I reply.

He pauses. "I suppose you have an explanation for both your absence and lack of contact?"

"I do." I make a face, grateful that the office is empty and Ouranos isn't standing in front of me. "The marina suffered an incident. And with it, transportation on and off this island."

He doesn't respond.

"And, unfortunately, my phone was on the boat. I suspect it's keeping the fish company now."

"Your plan?" he clips out.

"Wait for the coast guard to clear the area and get a ferry in here. Get the fuck off this island."

Ouranos sighs. "You're valuable, Kade, but I do hope you know that lying makes my skin crawl. What aren't you saying?"

I shift in the chair. Since I met him, he's had the

uncanny ability to see through people. There's never any use lying—he'll catch it. And apparently, that's also true for phone calls.

"There's been a development with my sister." I leave the rest hanging, unsure if Ouranos would let that information slip to Gabriel.

I kind of doubt it—he's not known for spilling secrets unless it serves him. However, this secret *might* serve him. It could unravel Gabriel even more.

"Your sibling has fully distracted you." His voice is hard. "Meanwhile, you have not found the man who killed my brother."

Saint Hart.

Found him, nearly stole him away. Kissed him.

Thought about fucking him...

Thought about fucking him while he fucks Artemis.

My mind spiraled, but whatever. I've never been with a man *and* woman before. The only complicating factor is that Saint can't seem to stand her at the moment.

"I expect results," Ouranos says when I don't reply. "Distractions aside—you know your job."

"I do. And..." I hesitate. "I'm sorry. I'll be back as soon as I'm able."

"See that you are."

Click.

The line goes dead in my ear, but I'm slower to set the phone back on its receiver. I pick it right back up and dial again. Unsurprisingly, it goes straight to voicemail. An automated voice reads out the number, then prompts me to leave a message.

"I'm in paradise," I say. "My phone's out of commission, but don't call this one back. There's nothing new to report. I'll be back to Sterling Falls soon."

I hang up and head back to Lyssa's room, checking that she's still asleep. There's no sign of Dr. Hawthorne or anyone else, and my stomach cramps. It's only then that I register the dark sky and how late it's gotten.

I spent the whole day here.

Shaking my head, vaguely annoyed at myself, I grab my coat from the back of the chair in Lyssa's room and shrug it on.

The walk back to the cabin is cold. It starts off relatively refreshing, the frozen air prickling my lungs with every deep inhale. Warm clouds billow out in front of me on my exhales. Snowflakes begin to fall, and my shoulders and head are blanketed in a dusting of white powder by the time I climb the porch steps and stamp my boots.

From the windows emanates a low, flickering light. There was smoke coming from the chimney.

Good to know one of them is competent enough to start a fire.

I let myself in and kick off my boots, finding them all in the living room. Reese has the chair, Artemis is sprawled on one side of the couch, and Saint takes up the other side. Not the formation I expected, given Saint's attitude.

They all look over at me.

"Just in time," Artemis says. "We were going to send out a search party."

A smile ghosts my lips. "Were you?"

"No," she admits. "We were going to start cooking dinner, though."

My stomach lets out another unfortunately timed growl.

"Careful," Reese laughs. "Kade gets hangry. He might be worse than Saint."

Saint's nostrils flare. "I don't—"

"You definitely do." Artemis sits up straighter. The blanket on her lap shifts, revealing the smooth, golden skin of her upper leg. No pants—there's tight fabric visible. Briefs, perhaps. "Pizza?"

I narrow my eyes at Saint's disgusted expression. "You don't like pizza, Hart?"

He jerks around. "It's not my favorite."

I shake my head. "Only psychopaths don't like pizza."

Reese bursts out laughing, and Artemis slaps her thigh. She points at me, an uncharacteristically relaxed smile curving her lips. "See? He *gets* it."

My chest swells. It seems they've had this conversation before, and I passed some unspoken test. I shake it off, not wanting to seem excited by that fact, and head into the kitchen. I was gone by the time Saint and Reese came back from town with supplies.

"Any problems?" I call.

"Nope," Reese replies. His footsteps signal his approach, and he leans against the edge of the counter while I examine what's in the fridge. "Plenty of gossip about what happened. So far, no one's connecting that it was on purpose. They think it was an accident that got out of control."

I snort. People are so... *innocent*. Or maybe naive is a better word. It's easier for them to believe that a bunch of boats just happened to blow up—along with the docks and the whole infrastructure of the marina—than to consider that someone violent is among them.

"Should make it easier to get out of here when they clear the area," he adds.

"Back to Sterling Falls?"

Reese inches closer. He puts a palm to the fridge door and closes it, so there's nothing between us. "We're going to stop Ouranos, brother."

Brother. Gabriel calls me that, sometimes. But I believe it more coming from Reese. We've known each other longer, been through war together. *Literally*. We've fought together.

"I see the gears in your head spinning." Reese stares at me. "Help us."

My mouth opens and closes.

"If you won't switch sides, at least give us something to make it a fair fight."

They don't know Ouranos. They might research him, track down his history, but it's one thing reading about it and another entirely to understand the man who lived it. Fighting him is like fighting a mountain.

He'll bury them without a thought.

"ATLAS," Artemis says suddenly.

Our food is gone—Kade found two frozen pizzas I had grabbed on a whim and cooked them for us—but our bellies are full. I've been staring at the fire for the past few minutes, zoning out and trying not to let my eyes shut.

Now, I refocus on her.

Kade and Saint are watching her, too.

Artemis looks to Kade. "Why Atlas?"

"Atlas?"

Artemis barely glances at Saint to explain, "Kade first showed up at Olympus. Black outfit. Black mask. Said he was there as Atlas."

Saint seems intrigued by that.

"So my question is..." She drags her index finger around the rim of her wine glass. She hasn't drunk much of it. A sip or two at most, probably just to be polite. She's more of a whiskey gal. "What made you choose him?"

Kade leans forward and braces his elbows on his thighs. "You know him, don't you?"

"He holds the sky on his shoulders," she says.

"Yes, but *why?*"

Saint eyes him, and his face pales. He says on an exhale, "Punishment."

Kade nods slowly.

Fuck. I'm totally lost. I turn to Artemis for help, and she seems equally shocked.

"Atlas, in Greek Mythology, was punished after participating in the war against the Olympians," she tells me. "So... you were saying, even then, not to trust you?"

Kade nods. "Subtle, hmm?"

"It probably explains Jace's hostility," she mumbles. "He's a whiz at that sort of thing."

"What made you think of that?" Saint asks.

Artemis hesitates, then says, "No reason."

"Bullshit." Saint immediately jumps on the slip. "What is it?"

"Can you not jump down my throat all the damn time?" she snaps.

I clench my jaw, waiting for Saint's next move. They need to work out their issues—and me stepping in to help or defend her every time doesn't *help*. It just puts up a barrier.

Besides, Tem is perfectly capable of handling herself. And Saint's asshole behavior.

"You're a hypocrite," Saint seethes. "You keep telling me to try and remember—"

"No, I definitely haven't said *that*, but you wouldn't

know since you never listen to a damn word I say." Tem shifts onto her knees on the couch. "Your memory going away just turned you into the same douche canoe I've known for the last year. Big change of events."

My eyebrows inch higher. Saint only rises to Tem's bait—or maybe it's the other way around.

"You're purposefully withholding things that could *help* me," Saint barks. "You don't explain anything! You just wag your finger at me like I'm some fucking disappointment."

"You *are* a disappointment!" She shakes her head. "And some things are better left unspoken."

Like how he fell in love with her?

"God, I understand why we didn't get along." Saint screws up his face in disgust. "If you acted like this all the time."

"Enough." Kade's voice slices through their argument. His gaze locks on Saint. "She's protecting you. She's always protecting you."

Oh, how the tides turn. Kade's expression is intense, completely serious, and all his body language is zeroed in on Saint.

Hell, I've been on the receiving end of a similar look. Just, you know, without the sexual tension behind it, too. It's hard not to fold when he gets like that.

A flush works its way up Saint's neck. He's clearly feeling the effects.

Artemis rolls her eyes at them, the conversation—err, argument—clearly over for the moment. She returns to her position, flinging the blanket back on her lap. She sets the wine aside, and it's hard to miss how her fingers linger at the crook of her elbow.

Guilt worms through me at all the signs of her addiction we didn't see.

"It's going to be different when we go back," I say in a low voice.

Her head whips around.

I focus on her hand, then switch back to her warm brown eyes.

She bites her lip and carefully nods.

My burner phone buzzes in my pocket. I picked one up while Saint and I were in town, and my one text was to Daniel so he could connect me with everyone. I slide it out now and scan the text.

Daniel: 911. Call me.

I jump to my feet and hit the button to dial him back, striding out of the room. I don't know where to go, just that I'm not a hundred percent sure Kade should overhead whatever I'm about to say.

"Reese?" Daniel asks.

I roll my eyes. "Yes. Obviously."

"Not obviously. Quick: who did you ask the Olympians to rescue in Emerald Cove?"

"An old friend." I narrow my eyes. "Do I need to elaborate?"

"No, that is acceptable. I'm passing you over to Jace King."

I end up in Kade's room. Well, Tem's room, I suppose.

"This is Jace," a deep baritone voice says a moment later. "We're sending a boat for you, Artemis, and Saint."

My body tenses. "Why?"

"There's been a new development—it seems that Gabriel knows where you are."

I stare off into the middle distance. The room is dark, but outside is awash with the almost gray luminance of falling snow. "I imagine that's a problem."

"Saint killed Ouranos' brother. We suspect Gabriel or Kade have been given orders to bring him in. And now that our hiding place has been uncovered, it's best you all return on your own terms."

I swallow. I can't say I know Jace—hell, he still lands squarely in the *stranger* category. The only reason I trust what he's saying are the stories I heard during my time spent with Daniel and Saint—before the amnesia accident—plus, he's considered Tem's family. That automatically gives him some points.

"When?"

"Boat's on its way."

"You didn't happen to hear about the marina exploding, did you?"

He pauses, then lets out a huff. "Yeah, I heard about it. Wait—"

"Guilty."

He laughs. "Naturally. There's a private dock used by the trauma camp. It's probably where you dropped Saint off."

I nod to myself. "I know it."

"Meet the boat there in thirty minutes."

Ah, fuck. I guess he doesn't give a shit about whoever's out there guarding it while the island is on lockdown.

I can sense he's ready to end the call. I blurt out, "Wait—"

"Yeah?"

"How many people can the boat hold?"

24 ARTEMIS

THIS IS INSANE.

Insane.

Kade had a cache of weapons locked in a safe, but he refused to give me a gun. He refused to give Saint one either. Mumbled something about us shooting each other. Instead, he and Reese loaded up, then we piled on every piece of dark clothing we could find and spent time locking down the cabin.

Then, we split up.

I follow Kade toward the trauma camp. Reese and Saint are going to scope out the dock to clear us a path, but there's one extra factor involved.

Lyssa.

Kade's face turned stony when Reese came back in the room and told him what he'd discovered. That Gabriel had found out about where we are, that Ouranos is out for Saint's blood...

Good stuff.

"I didn't tell him anything," Kade says again, glancing back at me.

I roll my eyes. "You said."

"Well, it's the truth. He's caused enough havoc to last a lifetime."

Also true.

Our mission? Hide Lyssa.

We can't remove her from Isle of Paradise, but we *can* make it look like she was moved.

Dr. Hawthorne meets us at the edge of the trees. She leads us around to a building I've only gone in once, for a tour of the place when I first arrived: the locked unit. It's for those who are a bit more emotionally unstable.

There are more orderlies on shift twenty-four seven, private rooms, and additional support staff for each patient.

Resident.

Whatever.

"We've moved her already," Dr. Hawthorne says. "And issued new paperwork. As of tonight, she's Lisa Jones, admitted a week and a half ago for psychosis treatment and physical therapy."

Kade frowns.

It doesn't sound nice...

"And Lyssa's files?"

"Will say she was discharged into your care," Dr. Hawthorne confirms. She pauses. "I assume I can do the same for Saint Hart?"

I nod.

"Just know that you can come back at any time." She touches my shoulder. "Or call. If you need it."

Kade clears his throat. "We're on a time crunch here, Doc."

She dips her chin and continues down the hall and stops outside a closed door. She uses her ID to unlock it and waves us ahead.

I stay in the hall—*call me paranoid*—while Kade goes in. His voice mingles with Lyssa's confused, sleepy one. He explains about moving her for her safety, for the name change... He apologizes, then leaves.

Dr. Hawthorne closes the door firmly behind him and folds her arms over her chest. "This is it, then? Getting off the island no matter what?"

Kade shifts. "Next time we can dive into my claustrophobia, Doc. Next time."

She chuckles.

We leave her behind and meet Reese and Saint in the woods. It's relatively easy to find them, since they're right off the path. We would've tripped over them if they were any less obvious.

"Two guards," Reese reports. "No perimeter as far as I can tell. Just the Coast Guard dingy docked there."

"Easy enough to sabotage," Saint murmurs. "Slice it and sink it."

Kade nods his approval. "And the guards?"

"Sneak attack. Incapacitate long enough to get away," Reese advises.

"Good." Kade points at me and Saint. "Stay."

I frown.

Saint seems just as annoyed.

But, since neither of us have weapons, we do as we're told and watch them silently disappear into the shadows.

"This is fun," Saint gripes. "I don't understand half of what's happening anymore."

"You killed someone's brother. That someone is now invading Sterling Falls and calling all the shots." I eye him. "The brother was Kronos, for the record. He's the one who slit Nyx's throat."

Saint's expression blanks. It does that sometimes, although I can't tell if he does it to suppress emotion or memory.

Maybe both.

I ignore it until Reese shines a light in our direction, flashing it twice.

We hurry down to the dock, and the familiar sound of water lapping against the shore gives me a modicum of peace.

Then again, this *is* where Saint pushed me into the frigid water and nearly let me die of hypothermia...

Maybe he didn't mean it.

Maybe he did.

He jumped in after me and carried me back, though, so that's a plus.

Still, I inch away from him and closer to Reese. We stand at the edge of the dock, and Kade allows Saint the honor of stabbing the dingy. It takes some time to deflate enough to let water in, but Saint knows his way around a knife. Before long, it's completely submerged.

"I thought you were going to get Lyssa," Reese says to me.

"Too risky in her condition. She needs professionals to help jumpstart her body again." I tilt my head. "But when Gabriel comes looking, it'll seem like we moved her off the island."

Reese smiles. "Sounds like something that might cause him to come unglued."

"I know." I smile back. "I feel like we already saw so much of his bad side... but the worst is yet to come. And this time, we have the leverage."

Take out Gabriel, take out Kade, and who does Ouranos have left who he trusts?

Hopefully—no one.

That's how we'll win this war.

PART 2

25   ARTEMIS

STERLING FALLS FEELS DIFFERENT. I can't put my finger on it, but even just standing on the porch of my brother's house, it's like...

"Smoke."

I glance over my shoulder.

My brother stands in the shadows, his arms crossed. He's been watching me more than usual since we arrived a few nights ago.

Don't get me wrong—the reunion was nice. Flinging myself into his embrace and just *breathing* for a moment, with the person who's known me since birth, settled something inside me.

"Smoke," I repeat, my brows furrowing.

"The Cyclopes have been enjoying a free reign of terror. They use fire as an intimidation tactic." He steps up beside me.

I swallow his words. Digest them. "Sterling Falls is burning?"

That can't be allowed to continue. I slide my hand into my brother's, squeezing softly.

"This needs to end."

He exhales. "And somehow, I fear it's only beginning."

———

THE HOUSE IS BURSTING at the seams with people. Apollo, Jace, Wolfe, and Kora live here, and all four have returned from Emerald Cove. I guess there was an argument for Kora to stay away, but she put her foot down. She returned with her guys, along with the person Reese tasked them with saving. She has been elusive, hiding in one of the bedrooms upstairs.

Because of that, I haven't seen her. I didn't ask what situation they pulled her out of, and my capacity for it is low—unsurprisingly.

Antonio and Vittoria are here, as well.

Plus Reese, Saint, and Daniel.

And Kade.

My stomach twists. I'm not exactly sure I can count Kade as a houseguest... he's currently locked in the basement.

Untrustworthy, and all of that.

I didn't put him in the basement. For the record. That was Jace and my brother, their faces stoic masks as soon as Kade climbed up the ladder from the small boat dock below. Kade, to his credit, didn't resist. He seemed resigned to it.

Wolfe and Daniel sit at the kitchen table. There's another, larger table in the dining room that we've been using for meals. Antonio and Vittoria have made themselves comfortable in the kitchen, preparing various meals.

"Where's Saint?" I ask.

Wolfe frowns. "Upstairs, maybe?"

Maybe.

I don't know why I asked—I had a bad feeling. *Have* a bad feeling. I go upstairs and pause outside the door to the room he's been sharing with Reese and Daniel. I've been sleeping on an air mattress in Antonio and Vittoria's room, leaving the mystery guest alone in the last guest room.

I knock. There's rustling, and after a moment, Reese pulls the door inward. He smiles when he sees me, stepping aside to allow me in.

He reaches out and brushes at my shoulder. "Is it snowing?"

"A bit."

"The droplets of water clinging to your hair say otherwise."

I frown. I guess I was outside longer than I thought. It seems like the first flakes had only just begun to fall when I stood up from the edge of the cliff wall and made my way back. The sky is gray this morning, the water a churning, white-capped midnight blue.

It's not water I would want to jump into, even from an easy height like this.

"I was hoping to find Saint." I look around the room. "He's not hiding in the closet, is he?"

Reese smirks. "Literally? No."

My cheeks heat. "Okay. Well..."

I back out of the room, leaving him to... whatever he was doing. With a quick shake of my head, I pivot away.

But that does give me an idea as to where Saint has slunk off to. Anger spikes through me. I rush downstairs, to the basement door that should be locked. It swings open easily.

Damn it, Saint.

I keep my footsteps light, my restraint barely holding on, and make my way silently into the basement. It's divided into a few rooms, only one of which my brother and his partners have done anything about. There's a couch and a few chairs facing a wall-mounted television, game controllers strewn around, and a fridge tucked off to the side that I suspect holds mainly beer. I bypass that and the door to the laundry room, pausing outside the room where they're holding Kade.

To be fair—it is set up to be a bedroom. I caught a glimpse when I followed them down on our arrival and spotted a mattress on the floor, sheets and blankets folded on the end of it with a pillow, and an open doorway to a small bathroom.

The door is shut, but voices drift out from under it.

Kade wouldn't be talking to himself, which means— *ding, ding, ding*—I've found Saint.

I grit my teeth against the sudden wave of anger that heats my skin.

I twist the knob and shove, bursting into the room. I half expect to catch them doing something they shouldn't, but... no.

Kade sits on the edge of the bed, his long torso leaned back, propped on his hands. His legs are spread wide, but he's fully clothed.

Saint stands by the half-sized window in the far corner. The lights are off, and that glass provides the only light source. It's too much like Terror for my liking. The room, the high window...

At least there's a bed in here. Access to a bathroom.

Oh, and no one is making Kade perform sexually against his will.

"What are you doing in here?" I ask Saint.

He rolls his eyes. "Talking."

"Saint," Kade says in a low voice. His tone...

Saint's shoulders hike up. "Sorry, Artemis. I came down here to see what else Kade could fill in for me."

My gaze bounces from Saint to Kade. The latter seems unsurprised by my entrance, and he scoots to the side, then pats the empty space next to him.

"You shouldn't manipulate him," I tell Kade. "You can't just twist his head up into knots."

Neither of them has a reply, and Saint makes no move to leave. So... I take the bait and sit next to Kade.

Like this, his height is much more apparent. His shoulder is even with my forehead, and I have to crane back just to see his face. I pivot to face him and bring my leg up on the bed.

"I wasn't trying to manipulate him." Kade examines

his fingernails on one hand. "He came to me. I'm the one locked down here."

"Which means you'd have motive *to* manipulate," I argue. "What were you saying?"

"I wanted to understand how we met," Saint says. "Up until a few days ago, I was certain I was straight. And now..."

"I was in the process of telling him about my naked ocean swims," Kade adds. "And how you two interrupted me. That's how you knew about my piercings, by the way. You saw it with your own eyes."

"And turned a lovely shade of red," I murmur.

Kade cracks a smile.

"So did you, Tem."

Great.

"Well." I clear my throat. "That answers that."

"I have another question," Saint says. He scratches at his jaw. "You care for your sister. It seems clear that you care, at least in part, for Artemis and me."

Kade nods slowly. "I do."

"So what loyalty do you owe Ouranos? Why continue to help him when he's hurting our city? And us, by extension?"

That's a good question, Saint.

The conversation from the cabin comes back to me. Kade picked Atlas because, on some level, he thinks he deserves punishment for taking up this war against the Olympians. And, presumably, Sterling Falls in general.

Kade already feels remorse. He's been trying to protect us from the start, hasn't he? The Cyclops sweatshirt he thought would send a message to keep me safe on the streets, his warning to Saint to get Antonio out when Ouranos arrived...

Not that Saint *remembers*. Maybe fragments. Feelings. There's got to be something there, right?

He's locked in on Kade, and he steps closer when Kade remains silent. His expression is something fierce. "Ouranos wants to extinguish everything that gives this town its charm. The small businesses are burning. Who do you think those belong to? Gang members and criminals? No. Innocent Sterling Falls folks who have been through enough war. What about my tattoo shop? Antonio's restaurant? Tem's club? All the work we put into making this place *good*, Ouranos waves his hand and his guys destroy it. I may have forgotten how we met, Kade, but I still know and love Sterling Falls. Ouranos wants to burn it to the ground—and you're complicit in that."

I rise. Kade's attention drops to the floor and stays there, and the muscle in his jaw jumps. Whatever the answers are, they seem locked in his head. More punishment? Self-inflicted, this time.

I hold my hand out to Saint. "Come on. He'll answer in his own time."

Saint sighs, but he doesn't protest. He comes forward and takes my hand, and my heart skips. His skin is cool and rough against my hot palm, and it takes everything in me to not squeeze tighter.

Willing contact has to be a step in the right direction...

I don't waste time lingering. I pull Saint out of the

room, only pausing to let him close the door and lock it behind us.

"YOU CANNOT GO."

I burst out laughing. The sentence is so funny—so unusual and unexpected—my stomach cramps. I double over, still howling. Tears leak from the corners of my eyes.

"Not right now," he amends.

The humor seeps from me. I straighten, blinking rapidly. "You weren't joking?"

Ouranos looks at me blankly and doesn't answer.

I stiffen. "The one thing I care about—and you'll deny me?"

He sighs. He sits on his throne—a booth along the back wall of his bar—and swirls the whiskey in his glass. It must be a little demeaning to slide his bum across the leather to remove himself from it. I think I'd like to see that, just to get a snicker in. But *right now* is no laughing matter.

I spin away abruptly, pacing the length of the empty

bar. The stools are all tucked away, the booths wiped down. Everything in this wretched place is so *tidy*.

Enough of that. I plant my hands on the bar top and spring up, hopping over with ease. I land amongst the liquor bottles and glasses, the empty chest that will hold ice when this place opens.

If it opens.

The bartender comes out from the back and stops short.

I pick up a bottle of whiskey. "How much does this cost?"

The bartender glances at his boss, then back at me. "For you, sir? N-nothing."

"Oh, goodie." I twist off the cap and upend the bottle. The amber liquid splashes the rubber mat under my feet, droplets getting on my boots. It goes and goes, until there's nothing left. I pivot and whip it across the room, and the bottle shatters on the far wall.

I crack my neck and grab another bottle. Vodka.

"This one?"

"I—"

"It's only a tantrum," Ouranos interrupts. "You may leave us."

The bartender turns and flees. I chuck the bottle at his head, and it explodes against the doorframe just beside him. He gives a yelp and moves faster, disappearing from view.

Pity.

"Are you about done?" Ouranos asks.

I find the glasses, all in neat rows, and fling them to the floor.

Shards everywhere.

There's a baseball bat under here, too. For unruly guests? It has a nice weight to it. I bounce it up and down, my grip firm, then heft it. It slips from my grasp and flies into the shelves of liquor. It breaks more than a few, knocks some loose, the glass shelving cracks. Everything is so *unstable*. One rogue person...

"Enough."

I tilt my head, ignoring that his voice is suddenly a lot closer. He's not over the bar, yet, but I think I could push him into that. I smile to myself and pick up the bat again, this time keeping a hold of it when I swing. It has a *lot* more power that way.

"My parents didn't get me into sports," I say. I lift the bat over my head and bring it down straight in front of me. "Never got to toss a ball with dear ol' dad—*oof.*"

Ouranos catches the back of my neck and shoves me down with surprising strength. My cheek cracks into the counter, bits of glass slicing my skin. The pain isn't off-putting. I've always welcomed it with open arms, and this time is no different. Not his firm grip, not the glass. Not the way my body contorts.

More, I want to shout.

"You work for me," Ouranos says in my ear. "You do what I say, when I say it. You do not defy orders simply because you think you know better—or because your time is more important than mine."

I exhale. "What are you ordering?"

"We have a new business venture. One you're decid-edly experienced in."

My eyebrows rise. "Torture?"

"No."

"Blowing things up?"

"*No.*"

I smack my lips. "Hmm. Um—"

"*Terror,*" he breathes. "You're going to help me get Terror back into working order."

I'm not used to fear. I stopped being afraid a long time ago. But now, it pulses through me. My heart thumps extra-hard, so much so that I wonder if Ouranos can feel it through his fingers.

He releases me and removes the bat from my hand. He moves away, exiting the bar by normal means. He returns to his booth, to his drink, and sips it idly. His gaze, however, returns to mine. His expression is sharp and expectant.

"I—" I wet my lips. My voice has deserted me.

Ouranos sighs, long and slow. "I was a patron, once upon a time. It was a marvelous place for those who needed a little... *extra.* For pleasure. A fascinating concept. A wonderful moneymaker. My brother got me in touch with the owner, and I was able to invest. It paid *dividends.* It put me where I am today. And, as the last investor, Terror rightfully belongs to me."

"And the part about needing revenge for your brother?"

He dips his chin. "A half-truth. Or, killing a couple birds with one stone. I take over Sterling Falls, I kill the man who murdered Wesley, and I bring Terror to its former glory."

I turn away. I need... *something*. Something beyond this conversation, beyond his plans. They swarm in my head, all his words like individual bees making a collective, dissonant buzz.

"I've overwhelmed you." Ouranos sighs. "Go, then. Slink off and regain control over your mind. And while you're at it—find Kade. His leash has been far too slack of late."

I manage to walk out the door. I keep my steps even, pace controlled down the sidewalk, and turn into the alley. I pause at my bike—*stolen bike*—and catch a glimpse of myself in one of the mirrors. The side of my face is bloody, and there are still bits of glass stuck to my skin.

The pain isn't there, though. It's secondary to the incessant buzzing.

I slide the helmet on and flip the visor down, obscuring my face.

Slink off and regain control. Seems he's always wanting me in one form or another, and it's never where I am.

Find Kade. My faithful sparring partner. He has no connection to Terror, but Artemis does. And Kade's little friend, Reese... he does, too.

I don't really care about finding Kade, but I need a distraction. Something to shut off this noise in my head. You cannot go—that's what he said. When I asked about Lyssa. Something is wrong, and I cannot go.

I cannot go. I cannot—

I slap myself.

It doesn't help. The helmet protects my face from any pain. I slap my head, over and over, trying to get the words to shut off. The buzzing gets louder. His voice gets louder.

Find Kade. Slink off. *You cannot go.*

My skin itches all over. There's something inside me that's getting worse and worse, and soon enough, I'll explode. I don't know what I'm going to do.

But then again—I never do.

27 SAINT

EVERY CHAIR around the dining table is taken. I glance from face to face—some deeply familiar, some becoming more so—and keep my expression blank. I idly pick at my fingernail, and while we wait for this *meeting* to start, my mind wanders back to Kade.

How he interacts with Tem is interesting. Revealing. He cares about her—his brows furrow a little when I make some remark toward her he doesn't like. He didn't resist the rough treatment from Jace, Apollo, and Wolfe, didn't say a single thing or make a *sound* when they showed him his new accommodations.

But if I scowl at Artemis? He looks at me funny.

She's diagonal to me, her gaze fixed on Wolfe. He's next to her, and he has her hand in his. Palm up. He's tracing some line and speaking to her in a low voice. Not sure what sort of bullshit he's spewing—something about life lines, maybe? Elora was big into that. She liked tarot cards and psychic readings and stars. But, spoiler alert: none of it means shit when you're at war.

Who would put stock in a crease in your palm? It's dumb.

Next to Wolfe is Kora. She seems familiar, and apparently we've had a lot of interaction over the last two years. I don't have a lot of memories with her, though. They were knocked out of my brain along with everything else. She's with all three of them—Apollo, Wolfe, Jace—and I think my eyes bugged out when they laid it out for me.

I mean, good for her. I couldn't have shared Elora...

Stop thinking about her.

On Tem's other side is Reese. Then Antonio and his wife, Vittoria. Both seem grim. Daniel sits beside me, with Apollo on my other side, and to his left is Jace at the head of the table. The girl they brought back from Emerald Cove is absent, still hiding upstairs. Kade is downstairs.

They're the only two in the house who *aren't* here.

Jace finally stands, his chair scraping the floor and effectively silencing the quiet conversations. "We are all in agreement that Ouranos, also known as Marcus Graves, needs to be stopped. Wolfe was able to connect with some of our contacts, but not nearly enough. Our information network is severely impaired, which means we're flying blind."

"What about the sheriff?" Daniel asks.

"Antonio told us that his sister, Nadine, is currently in a drug-induced coma." Jace's attention flicks to Artemis. "We don't know where he's keeping her, but I imagine it's somewhere close to him. He would want Bradshaw under his thumb completely, and forcing his cooperation by continually threatening his sister is a good start."

Artemis drums her fingers on the table. "Another thing: Malik is missing. The Hell Hounds will be fragmented without a leader."

All eyes turn to Wolfe. His father was the former leader of the Hell Hounds—I missed his demise, too—but when push came to shove, Wolfe wanted no part of the motorcycle gang.

Kora grips his hand tightly and gives him a small nod.

"Fine," Wolfe mutters. "I'll take that on. See who I can round up."

"The clubhouse is gone," Artemis adds. "You'll have to do a bit of digging."

"Okay." Jace nods. "Wolfe will find the remaining Hell Hounds, see if we can pull a bit of manpower."

"And where will you *put* them?" Antonio asks. "Surely not here."

"No," Wolfe answers immediately. "The new warehouse is still standing, surely?"

Daniel makes a face. He has his laptop open in front of him, and his fingers fly across the keyboard. He swivels it around for us to see an aerial view of South Falls. The building *is* still standing, if that's a current picture.

"The first was blown up," Apollo says under his breath. "About a year ago."

I grit my teeth. My head hurts. This planning doesn't really have anything to do with me, does it? I don't understand why I'm here. Same with Antonio and Vittoria. They're innocent. I can shoot a gun, at least, but I feel more like a soldier carrying out orders. Being around for the discussion seems wrong.

"I need some air," I whisper back.

I slip out of the room, my shoulders hunched. Part of me wants to go back to the basement and talk to Kade. The other wants to rush outside, to heave myself off the cliff and let the waves swallow me. It would at least put a physical feeling on this intense pressure all over my body.

Since that would probably freak people out, and I don't want a repeat of the hypothermia experience on the island—*your fault for pushing her*—I find myself going upstairs. To faceplant in bed? To bash my head against the wall?

The hallway isn't empty, and I stop in my tracks. A woman is at the far end, and she stops mid-step when she spots me. Her face is familiar.

I tilt my head, racking my brain. Why is it *familiar*?

"Saint Hart?"

"Yeah—"

She comes closer, tucking loose strands of her white-blonde hair behind her ear. "Do you remember me?"

I slowly shake my head. "I've been having some memory issues lately, though, so it's not just you."

She pauses in front of me. "Elodie St. Croix. I used to fight at Olympus as—"

"Hestia." I nod sharply as it comes back to me. She came around with her partner when Olympus was new, a fledgling operation. Hestia and... "You were a good fighter."

She fought Elora a time or two.

Her smile doesn't reach her eyes. "Yeah, well."

"How did you end up in Emerald Cove?"

Elodie curls her arms around her middle. She's in a dark-red sweatshirt and black joggers, and she swims in the amount of fabric on her frame. There's a green-and-yellow bruise under her jaw, and more little ones creating a ring around her throat.

"Long story," she says after a moment. "Not worth walking down that path again. Just know it wasn't a good one."

"But you met Reese somewhere along the way..." I glance over my shoulder. No one followed me, and the stairwell is empty. "You haven't talked to him yet?"

She frowns. "He's here?"

"He said he won a fight and used his favor to get you out of your situation." I shrug. "That's secondhand information. I was there but I have amnesia."

Her eyes widen. "Amnesia?"

"Weird, right?"

"The weirdest." She huffs. "I kind of wish I had amnesia."

"I'm sorry," I tell her. "Just know that this house is full of good people. You don't have to hide out up here. For whenever you feel like getting out of that room."

Elodie blinks rapidly and swipes at her eye. She shifts, turning away, and nods. "Thanks, Saint. I'm..."

She retreats. I watch her go, oddly at peace with that

conversation. I don't know what happened to her, but it was obviously something bad. And now she has a safe place to take refuge.

Well, as safe as you can get in a town that's in the middle of a hostile takeover.

"Saint."

I jump and whirl around. Artemis stands a few steps below me, her hands on the railing. Not on her hips. No accusation in her gaze. I make myself take note of that before I snap at her, which is my first instinct. There's something wrong about her expression that I can't put my finger on.

"What's wrong?" I ask.

Her shoulders hike. "Ouranos is taking everyone off the board. The Hell Hounds, the sheriff. He tried to remove my brother and his family by stopping them from returning to Sterling Falls. But..."

I squint at her. "You have an idea."

"Well, who's making all the moves for him? It's not a bunch of people—it's one person."

"Kade?"

She shakes her head. "No. Gabriel."

I laugh. I have yet to have the pleasure of that psycho's company, but I've heard tales from Reese. He's been filling me in the best he can, especially over the last few days. Sure, he wasn't around for the first gang war in Sterling Falls, and he didn't get a front-row seat to Jace, Wolfe, and Apollo falling in love with Kora. But he seems to have picked up on a lot, and he's been telling me about what's happened *since*.

One thing he couldn't stress enough was that Gabriel was a bad guy.

"So, you want to kill Gabriel?"

She rears back. "What? No!"

I pause. "Then…"

Artemis shakes her head. "Forget it. Of course you'd go straight to murder."

She spins on her heel and trots back down the stairs. She passes the dining room, which still has some lingering folks in it, and goes right out the door.

"Artemis, wait—"

Belatedly, I notice she's already wearing a coat. Her boots. I snatch mine at the door and shove my feet into them, then grab a jacket and follow her. She's making a beeline for the car parked under the trees. Because of the natural shelter, there's only a dusting of snow on it.

I reach her just as she slides into the driver's seat. The engine starts, and the windshield wipers turn on, clearing her view.

I stand in front of it for a second, then swear and go to the passenger-side door. I fold myself into the small frame with a grunt, staring straight ahead.

When nothing happens, I glance over.

She's staring at me.

"What?" I growl.

Her eyebrows hike. "Just wondering what possessed you to follow me."

"You can't go find Gabriel on your own." I cross my arms. "I've heard he's insane. And, plus, what if he tries to drug you? All that effort on Isle of Paradise, down the drain."

She grits her teeth. "Oh, yeah? How long have you been waiting to throw that in my face?"

Ah, hell. I blow out a breath. "That's not what I meant."

She twists to face me. "What *do* you mean?"

"Gabriel is dangerous. Addiction is no joke. I think..." I pinch the bridge of my nose. "You're strong enough to resist that carrot if he dangles it in front of you. But what if he grabs you and just *does it* without waiting? He's going to be angry about Lyssa. Getting you dependent on him would be a way for him to exert control over a situation in which he currently has no control."

She blinks at me for a solid ten seconds, then nods briskly. "You're right. That's a possibility I hadn't considered."

Oh.

She twists the knob on the blowers, cranking the heat, and faces forward again. Her seat belt is already in place, and she puts the car in drive without another word.

"You'll be backup," she says. "Just don't kill him. I worked too hard to rescue him the first time."

"Wait—" I scoff. "No. Is this a *rescue* mission?"

She hits the gas. "Or an abduction. I haven't decided yet."

28   ARTEMIS

SAINT IS COMING WITH ME.

Saint willingly got in my car.

Well, not *my* car, but the car that I am borrowing without permission from Vittoria. Stealing, in other words. But I'm going to return it, so whatever we classify my usage as is just semantics.

It's not snowing anymore, and the roads are clearer than I expected. Still, as soon as I turn out of the driveway, I have a hard time not hunching forward and attempting to appear smaller.

"There's a gun in the glovebox," I say.

He flinches, then nods and leans forward. He pulls the handgun out and checks that it's loaded. He doesn't ask whose it is—at this point, I don't know that it really matters. Apollo took the opportunity to stash weapons everywhere. There's probably another one under the driver's seat, actually.

The real question is: where am I going to find Gabriel?

I drive north toward Olympus. Saint seems to get more restless the closer we get, until we crest the final hill and it comes into view. There's a wall along the road, with a gate at the entrance. The whole property isn't fenced—never was—so the gate was more of a stylish thing than anything else.

The gates hang open, one of them at an angle, hanging on by a single hinge, and bent like it was struck by a heavy vehicle.

Olympus itself appears okay—it's not on fire anyway.

"Are you…"

I turn into the driveway. The car squeezes through the gap between the gates. I drive past the building's grand main entrance, to the hidden door that will allow us in the back way. Besides, if anyone is patrolling, it would be better for them to not see a random car outside.

Once it's out of sight, we hop out. I fumble for the hidden handgun under my seat and check it, then tuck it into the waistband of my jeans.

Saint points at the clear tire tracks left in the snow. "Not conspicuous at all."

I shrug. "Best I could do."

He sighs. "Let me go first."

"Oh, since when did you become a gentleman?"

Saint scowls. It almost brings me a sense of comfort. He moves past me, gun held close to his body and aimed at the ground, one hand on the doorknob. Before opening it, he freezes. His attention moves to the cliffs.

"What?" I whisper.

He makes a face. "We jump off that together?"

"A few times." I roll my eyes. "You tackled me off it once."

To my utter shock, he smiles.

Smiles.

My breath stalls. I forgot what it's like when Saint Hart smiles.

Okay, I didn't forget—I purposefully blocked it out once I realized he had amnesia. And yes, he's smiled at others since then. He's let his whole face light up for other people. But this one is directed at *me*, and now my lungs aren't working.

"You must've really pissed me off." His tone is light.

I'm having an aneurism. Right? That would explain it.

"Okay," Saint says. "Let's go."

Freaking whiplash. He opens the door in a smooth movement and enters fast, gun up and at the ready. He clears the room, and I follow close behind him. He doesn't have military experience, which makes me wonder if Reese or Kade has been giving him tips. Or maybe he always had this knowledge and I just never asked.

We reach the hallway. It has open arches that allow a view into the main room. It's all dark, minus thin streams of light that come in through the upper windows. Our eyes adjust to the gloom, and we move forward together. Our footsteps are near-silent.

He holds up his hand, and we pause. He taps his ear.

I hear it, too.

A voice. I strain to listen, but I can only catch snatches of it.

"...can't do it, but he doesn't know what I can do. So just tell me..."

Saint glances back at me. I meet his gaze, eyes wide. It *sounds* like Gabriel, that's for sure. But it also sounds like he's not alone, which is worrisome.

There's nowhere to go but forward. Back isn't an option, not if we want to end this sooner rather than later.

"Go," I mouth.

Saint makes a face, but he listens and continues. We creep down the hall, passing each arch in a crouch. Gabriel finally comes into view at the third opening. He's on the platform where the fights take place, sitting on the edge. His feet swing. There's a glint of a knife in his hand.

There's someone else on the floor in front of him.

"Please," the *someone else* sobs. They're facedown, hands behind their back. When Gabriel doesn't reply, they try to shuffle away.

"That's not very nice." Gabriel hops down and grabs their foot. He drags them backward, closer to the plat-form. To their original spot.

"Lights," I whisper to Saint, my voice barely audible. I gesture back the way we came.

He scowls.

Of course he does.

But he seems to know that he's only here for backup, and this is *my* plan, because after a beat, he moves away. I take his position and peer around the column into the gloom. I can't tell who Gabriel has. Malik, perhaps? The shadowed figure appears male. Large, too, even though Gabriel moved him with ease.

I ball my fists, then force myself to relax. I need to focus on the task at hand and not anything else. Like, for example, Saint mentioning my addiction. Being concerned about me falling off the wagon—or being hauled off it, more like.

Now, naturally, it's in the back of my head. Not just that Gabriel is the dangerous connection to that part of me, but the drug itself. The rush of it hitting my vein, followed by the blistering after-burn.

Snap out of it.

"I don't know anything," the man groans. "I told you—"

The lights come on, all suddenly blazing.

Gabriel squints, lifting his hand.

That's my cue. I step out from my hiding spot and into the room.

He spots me immediately, but he doesn't seem surprised at all. He *claps.*

"Artemis! You're back." He moves away from the man and toward me.

I raise my gun automatically.

"Oh, wow." He sighs and stops. "Okay, fine. I suppose I deserve that. You seem good. Clear and sober, then?"

"Yes," I bite out. "But—"

"No, no, I know that's not why you're here. I don't

even have any of that filthy drug on me. No syringes for my little pet." He grins. "You've kicked the habit. I'm proud of you."

I clench my teeth. I should stash my gun, get closer. Tell him what I really came for. But now that the lights are on, I can clearly make out his hostage.

Sheriff Bradshaw.

"Damn it, Gabriel." Now I *do* put away my gun. "What are you doing with him?"

Nate looks *rough*. Two black eyes, his nose swollen and crooked—definitely broken. He has a split lip, and there's blood pooling under his body that wasn't visible in the dark. I'd guess he has some sort of wound in his gut—a stab or gunshot?

"I'm practicing the proper interrogation technique." Gabriel circles him and crouches on the far side. He grips the sheriff's hair and forces his head up. He tilts his face in my direction. "She's come to save you, isn't that sweet?"

I frown.

"Oh? Lookie." Gabriel's voice is gleeful. "She *didn't* come here for you. She came for... Olympus? Stumbled upon us? My mistake, putting you somewhere so discoverable."

"I came to talk to you," I say as evenly as I can.

"About?"

"About your master."

Gabriel physically recoils.

I nod slowly. "That's right—Ouranos. The one pulling all your strings."

"He doesn't pull my strings."

I scoff. "Yeah, he does."

He jumps to his feet and points at me. "No, he doesn't!"

"You and I both know that you'd already be on Isle of Paradise if he didn't." I plant my hands on my hips. "The boy I knew would never let someone tear him away from her. And you know something happened—yet, here you are. Taking out your frustrations on Bradshaw."

For a moment, I just stare at Gabriel. His dark hair is longer than I last remember. Pieces fall across his forehead and into his eyes. He drags his fingers through it intermittently, almost like a tic. He wears black pants, black boots, and an army-green long-sleeve shirt. No visible weapons.

That doesn't lend me any comfort.

There's no gun holstered at his hip, no knife—unless it's tucked in his boot, under his pant leg. That's where I would keep one.

His skin is still so pale. There are dark circles under his eyes. And there's a smattering of bruises across his cheek, as well as fresh cuts.

"What happened to you?" I ask.

He laughs. His dark eyes glitter. "You'll have to be more specific, Artemis. A lot has happened to me."

"Recently. To your face."

"Oh." He sighs. His whole body seems to cave in. "A little disagreement."

"And you were put in your place," I fill in. "With your face under his boot."

He perks, like my reason for being here suddenly makes sense. "What a nice play! You want to pit me against him."

I sigh. "I just want you to be *free*."

He locks up again.

Why?

Tension rolls through him, and he bursts into motion. He paces, his head bent. His gaze stays on his fingers, picking at his nails. "Freedom. Do you know what freedom means as a concept? It's just a bigger cage. More room to move around. The bars are a different color. But they're still there. It's all a trap. You can't believe in freedom because it's a myth. As impossible to reach as Heaven."

"No."

He jerks. "*Yes*, Artemis. You freed me, and now I am on a leash. I can roam, but I cannot do as I please. You free Lyssa, and she is trapped in her head. You freed Reese—well, I suppose Kade freed Reese Avery from a cage of *my* making—but he won't leave because he loves you. That's a cage all on its own, isn't it? Sooner or later, he'll gnaw off his own leg just to be free of you."

"Enough." Saint's voice cracks across the room like a whip.

Gabriel jumps and whirls. He spots Saint on the opposite side of the platform. His gun, unlike mine, is in his grip. It's up, pointed at Gabriel, and he doesn't seem at all conflicted about pulling the trigger.

"You know about love, don't you, Gabriel? Do you want to chew off your leg, to use your metaphor, to be free of Lyssa?" Saint skirts the platform and comes to a stop beside me.

Gabriel waves his hand. "She's different."

"Why? Because she's been gone the last ten years?" Saint glowers at him. "She's still alive, man. She's still here, and instead of being your best self for her, you've lost your damn marbles."

"Terror twists minds," Gabriel replies softly. "And wouldn't you know it? Terror is rising from the dead. I can already feel it. Do you think we expand to fit the cage we're in? How would it feel to be shoved back into the tiny box where fear began?"

A shiver sweeps down my spine. "Terror isn't coming back."

"Oh, yes, it is. That's his plan. Take the city, reignite Terror. He was an investor." Gabriel's eyes are wide, and he faces us. His hands come up, palms facing the ceiling. Like an open call for prayer. "And who are we? Entertainment. Bodies. Flesh to bleed and bruise and brutalize."

I glance at Saint. Ouranos wants to bring back Terror? That wasn't on my radar, but it *would* explain why he targeted Bow & Arrow so early on. My heart squeezes at the thought of my beloved club.

Did I build it on a literal shitstorm of trauma? Yes. But at the end of the day, that only made the work I was doing feel sweeter. I was able to employ a lot of people who were affected by human trafficking, and paying fair wages gave them a jumping-off point to a better life.

That means something.

It wasn't all for nothing. It was a frivolous decision.

"You'd help bring Terror back?" Saint asks.

Gabriel makes a vague choking noise. He waves off the question and focuses back on the sheriff. The pool of blood under Bradshaw is getting bigger, but he passed out at some point during our conversation. He's limp now, his cheek on the floor and his eyes shut.

"Doing nothing is just as bad as helping," I say. "You've already single-handedly taken every opposing player off the board for him. Who else is going to stop him? There's no one left."

He glares at me. "There's you."

I laugh. "Seriously?"

"Yes. The mighty Artemis. You stop him." He crouches and pokes Bradshaw in the side. Then again. "You go up against him and see how you fare."

I exhale. "Gabriel. Focus."

"What?" His gaze snaps to mine. "I am focusing on what I can control. Which, right now, is if the pretty sheriff lives or dies. He refuses to sing for me, so I'm leaning toward the latter. The amount of blood on the floor is staggering, isn't it? So much red for such a little cut."

"Help us," Saint says.

Gabriel's attention shifts again. He takes in Saint's face, the visible tattoos. He seems to analyze every part of him, then pushes up to his full height. He steps right over Nathan Bradshaw, his heel sliding in the blood, and approaches. They're pretty much the same height. While they're eye to eye, I marvel at the similarities between them. Minus the tattoos, and a bit of Saint's muscled frame, they may as well be brothers.

"Where'd you come from, Saint Hart?" Gabriel asks. "East Falls? A good family? Mommy and Daddy loved you, put you through the Sterling Falls school system. Did they watch with despair when you found this place? When you deviated from whatever their plan was? Or maybe they just turned away, moved far from this wretched place, and left you to your own devices. And you think that's so ugly of them, hmm? Poor, forgotten Saint. The prickly, scowly man who creates art for a living. Wasted talent, they probably said. You could've been an engineer! Or an astronaut! You could've flown so fucking far away from Sterling Falls.

"But you *didn't*. You stayed here and you rot because of it. You sat in classes in high school while I learned how to swallow rich semen. I washed filth off my skin every night, but it never really comes off. Does it, Artemis?"

I flinch.

Gabriel smiles at Saint. "Were you rough the first time you touched her? Did she convince you it doesn't matter that the bruises you left behind give her flashbacks of the men who paid to steal tastes of her skin? Shame."

"He's trying to get a rise out of you," I say to Saint. "And it doesn't matter either, because you can't remember it."

Saint cocks his head. He hasn't stopped staring at Gabriel, although his jaw works. The muscle there leaps with every clench of his jaw.

"*Can't* remember?" Gabriel inches closer, mirroring

Saint's head tilt. "Fascinating. I always wondered what it would be like to smash my brains in hard enough to forget my life."

"I used to, too," Saint murmurs.

I give him a look. He would've had no reason to think that way before Nyx died, right? Which means...

"We could do it again," Gabriel offers. "See if any of it comes back."

"It has been coming back." Saint scowls. "Gold dress. Whiskey. I was so fucking angry at her—"

"Oh, anger. Exciting. Keep going."

"I was cruel. Simple as that."

Gabriel pouts when Saint doesn't elaborate.

But then Saint narrows his eyes. "Do you regret meeting Lyssa?"

29 GABRIEL

I AM A BOY AGAIN. Gangly, awkward. My body aches. I stretch tall, my fingers burning on the glass bulb overhead. A quick twist, and it shuts off, encasing me in darkness. I dream of being free of this place. The room. The guards. The stage.

And then I blink, and I am back in Olympus. The stage here is different. It's a performance, yes, but it's not forced. Not yet.

I think Ouranos will move his operation here. He will let masked people enter, and instead of fights, they will watch sex as entertainment. Porn brought to life. There's brutality to it. There will be Terror, and then there will be *this* perversion.

The sheriff will be replaced. He's half-dead anyway. The knife went so far in, deeper than intended. I was just *angry*. Howling with madness.

Losing Lyssa unleashed a fury inside me that I haven't been able to quiet. Even when I am still, it twists and burns. She is not gone, as Saint so kindly pointed out, but she is as far from me as can be.

"I wish Reese were here," I say on a sigh. "He'd understand."

"Understand what?" Artemis asks.

Pretty Artemis, with her gold jewelry, her hair twisted back out of her face. It still flows down her back, the dark strands thick. Her skin has always been tanned, the olive undertones, her dark features. Lips and eyes and hair. She embodies the goddess she was named after. Her ancestors could've come from Greece or Turkey or Spain. Somewhere far, far removed from Sterling Falls.

"My parents sent me to Terror," I tell Saint. "They said the Devil lived in me. They said I was wicked."

Saint stands tall, but his expression belies his pity.

"*I am wicked!*" I shout. I pound my fist on the platform. "But I wasn't back then. As a child. I grew into this. I was made into *this*. Don't judge me for that, Artemis, you're just as much at fault as me."

She presses her lips together.

"Focus on Lyssa," Saint says softly. "Go back to her."

I am unholy. I am unsound.

The buzzing noise that's been in my head since Ouranos spoke of bringing Terror back to life only grows louder. I smack my head, but it doesn't do anything. It does remind me of the pain in my cheek. It took me ages to pick out the pieces of glass, and there might still be more. I got sick of bleeding on the floor.

I found Lyssa bleeding once. After we were sent down...

Down, down, down.

"Help us stop this," Artemis whispers.

I meet her eyes. She's so close. I have a tight grip on her arms, and she on mine. I don't remember moving. Didn't think about approaching. Just did it. Now, I can't let go.

"There's no bigger cage after this one, Gabriel. We can put an end to this, and you can be with Lyssa."

I narrow my eyes. "I spent the last decade waiting for her to wake up."

"Who's to say she won't?"

Do they know something I don't?

The noise ceases.

Silence.

There's silence in my brain and nothing else.

I take a breath, and it's all I hear. A sharp inhale.

A slow exhale.

My grip on Artemis tightens, but she doesn't flinch. She stares at me, eyes wide. That was her last bargaining chip, I reckon. So fucking *reasonable* of her.

And it's a good one.

The best one.

The only one that will work.

30 KADE

APOLLO AND ARTEMIS share similar features. Twins, of course, just like the gods of old. Apollo and I have already met—once at Olympus, masked, and again when he tried to warn me away from his sister. But that was a shadowed, dark affair. I wasn't analyzing.

Now, I'm outright staring.

Where Artemis has lean muscles and curves, Apollo has bulk. When he first escorted me down to the basement, he had scruff. Now, he's clean-shaven. His dark hair is short—impossible to tell if it's wavy like Tem's, but it seems thick enough.

Jace King sits across from me. Apollo is behind him, leaning against the wall. His arms are crossed.

Wolfe James stands at my shoulder, just out of reach. In case I decide to really fuck myself over and attack him, I guess. With bound hands.

The zip ties are overkill, but whatever. If it puts them more at ease...

Anyway.

"It was pitched to us that your loyalty could shift in our favor," Jace finally says.

Ah, that. Saint's plea. Did he mention it, or did Artemis?

I roll my shoulders back. "Loyalty is an interesting word."

"You're loyal to a madman," Apollo says.

"I *work* for a madman," I snap.

"Oh, you're on payroll? You get your taxes taken out like a good little employee?" Wolfe snickers.

"Taxes, 401-k, health insurance, the whole nine yards." I raise an eyebrow. "Does that make a difference?"

"Sure." Wolfe drags out the chair next to me and drops into it. He faces me, his knees nearly touching mine. "The *legal* way means Justice Marcus Graves isn't hiding who he's employing. But Daniel did a financial audit on you. He said there were no direct deposits into your accounts, no cashed checks.... Nothing that would indicate you work for him. Just monthly payments from the military after your medical discharge."

I nod slowly. "Guess that sounds about right."

"So you were being facetious," Jace clarifies.

"Obviously."

"How does he pay you?"

"Cash. An apartment. He promised me he would help me find Reese. That was the biggest thing."

Jace and Wolfe trade a look, but I can't read it. I don't speak their language. I've been holding on to this *loyalty* to Ouranos for so long. He made me rely on him, trust him. He carved out every bit of disobedience. Just like the military does.

It's similar, in a way. Their need for soldiers who will listen and follow commands, almost without question. Sure, there are questions. There will always be questions. But my ability to shove those aside and do what needed to be done...

My chest is tight. If they weren't watching my every move, I'd rub it. I'd press my fingers into the tattoo Saint gave me, the one he still doesn't know about. Is it so bad that I want him to remember it on his own?

The crunch of gravel outside precedes headlights shining through the windows. The car pulls past and rolls to a stop, the engine cutting off a second later.

I crane back and catch a glimpse of Saint and Artemis climbing out of it. Artemis goes for the porch while Saint circles around to the trunk. There, he pauses.

Waits.

He looks around and spots me through the glass. His brows furrow.

Tem bursts into the room, her sharp gaze immediately taking in the scene.

"Interrogating him without me?" Her voice is breathless.

Apollo shrugs. "Just talking."

"Yeah, right." She eyes me. "You good?"

I straighten in my seat and lift my zip-tied hands. "Peachy."

She scoffs. "Is that really necessary?"

"We don't know if we can trust him," Jace says evenly. "And he is a known fighter. This was just a safety precaution. What if he escaped and led the Cyclopes right back to us?"

"It's okay, Tem," I interject.

Apollo glowers at me.

Why? *Oh—her nickname.*

I clear my throat and shift. They don't know shit about my relationship to her. If she doesn't want me calling her that, she'd say it. And maybe she wouldn't say it with her voice, but her body language would absolutely translate it. So far, it hasn't.

Not that I've taken much opportunity to call her that anyway. Seemed like a wrong place, wrong time sort of deal.

"Where did you go?" Apollo asks her.

Exactly the question I wanted to ask.

She makes a face. "Negotiating."

Intriguing.

"With who?" her brother demands.

She gestures behind her. "Come and see."

Uh-oh.

Jace and Apollo immediately follow. Wolfe seems to contemplate, glancing from me to them, then finally grabs my arm and tugs me up.

"I'm not missing this for babysitting duty," he mutters.

I grin. "Fine by me."

He huffs. We step onto the porch just in time for

Saint to hit a button on the key. The trunk pops open, and he steps back quickly as a leg shoots out. My eyes bug out.

There's a person in there?

Saint stands back, arms crossed, as the person kicks in the air. Black pants, boots. Their legs pinwheel until their heels hook on the ledge of the trunk, and they use that to leverage themselves up and out.

I nearly choke when Gabriel rolls himself over the lip of the trunk and hits the ground feetfirst. He rises to his full height and straightens his shirt, patting his chest down. His hands, like mine, are zip tied.

What the hell have they done?

"And you were worried about me," I say to Wolfe under my breath.

He doesn't reply.

Gabriel looks around. When he lands on me, he smirks—then, noticing our similar predicament, the smirk transforms into a grin. "Twins, Kade! Always said we were brothers. Were you transported by trunk, too?"

"No—"

"Lovely way to travel." He eyes Saint. "I wonder if you decided to hit all the potholes along the way? Really gives the feel of a Russian massage."

"You haven't gotten a massage a day in your life," I say on a sigh.

"Oh. Well."

"I wasn't driving," Saint interjects.

Gabriel lights up. "That mayhem was *Tem*? I always knew she had spirit. Try as I might to break it..."

"Gabe—shut up."

He zeroes back in on me. "Don't call me Gabe."

I roll my eyes. "Don't call her Tem."

"Excuse me for wanting a bit of intimacy, *Kadius*."

"That's not even my name."

He pushes his shoulders back and steps away from the trunk. And Saint. He's quick-footed getting away from that one, which makes me wonder how calmly Gabriel got in the trunk. Probably not at all. He's got bruising on his cheek and deep gouges that should probably be checked out. Beyond that, there are dark shadows under his eyes and a bruise forming on his neck.

He circles the car and leans back, whistling softly. "Whose home?"

"Ours," Apollo bites out.

They know who he is. It's impossible not to—Gabriel has a terrible habit of making himself known. So why did Artemis choose to bring him here? And how the hell did they get him into the trunk?

Gabriel trots up the steps before anyone can stop him. He bypasses Wolfe and me and waltzes into the house.

"What the fuck, Tem?" Jace growls.

She shrugs and follows Gabriel.

"I don't suppose you're going to make us share the basement?" I ask. I follow her, escort be damned. She seems to have an idea, and no one else has any good plans. Why not see it through? "There's just one bed, and that would probably be awkward."

She doesn't respond.

Gabriel flops down on the couch and kicks his feet up on the coffee table. Honestly, he's worse than a child. He's feral.

Someone stops beside me, close enough that our arms touch. Out of the corner of my eye, I catch Saint's profile. It takes a lot of restraint to not smile.

Tem drops into the chair perpendicular to Gabriel. "Go on."

Gabriel heaves a sigh. "Oh, fine." He clears his throat. "Dear Artemis, I am so, so, so, so, so, so, so, so sorry for getting you addicted to heroin. It was not my intention at all—"

"Skip to the real part," she snaps.

He shifts a few times, nestling deeper into the cushions. "I would like to return to Isle of Paradise and lie down next to my love, close my eyes, and never wake up just like her. Maybe it would end the torment inside me. But for now—it seems Artemis has appealed to my sense of revenge. The only way I can fulfill my first desire would be to complete a task: to bring a crushing end to Ouranos."

I blink. "What?"

Gabriel meets my gaze. "Oh, Kade. You have to feel it, too, right? The disturbance? Something isn't right, and he won't let me go. I can't go see her. He said there's more important work to do."

Reese enters the room. He spots me first, confusion coloring his expression, then assesses the rest of the room like a good soldier. My stomach knots, and I nudge Saint.

My muscles tense, and I *watch* Reese spot Gabriel. The realization that crashes over him—and then the rage.

I'm already moving by the time Reese decides to act. I snap the zip ties—*it was only a matter of time*—and lunge for my friend. He has a gun in his hand. I catch his wrist and force it down, driving us backward.

The rest of the noise behind me is muffled. My heartbeat roars in my ears.

"Let go of me," Reese shouts. "He—"

"Stand down," I bark.

He fights me, but then Saint is there, too. He removes the gun from Reese's hand, and I pin my friend's shoulders to the wall at his back. He breathes heavily, jerking under my grip, but I have the weight and leverage to keep him there.

"Look at me."

Reese's wild gaze comes back to mine.

"He's bound. He was brought here in a fucking trunk."

"And if he escapes, he'll be the death of us all," he spits.

I cock my head. "You don't think that about me?"

"I—" His words die. "No, Kade. I don't know if I can trust you, but if you walked out of here? You wouldn't give us up."

I nod. *He's right.* I wouldn't.

"Artemis has a plan," Saint says at my shoulder. "I believe in her, and I think, if you can sit in the same room as that madman and hear what she has to say, you would, too."

Reese nods slowly, letting out a long exhale. His body relaxes.

"Just to be safe, though, Saint is gonna hang on to your weapon," I add.

He gives one more nod.

I release him and step back. When I turn around, Jace is behind us. His attention bounces around the three of us, and whatever he sees must pass his inspection. He steps aside, and we reenter the living room.

Gabriel's feet are off the coffee table, and a stern-looking Antonio hovers over him. That man is old but mighty. He has the face of a guy who has seen some shit—and that's coming from someone who has absolutely seen some shit.

"Oh." Artemis frowns. "We had to drop Bradshaw off at the hospital on the way over."

Jace makes a noise in the back of his throat. "Excuse me?"

"I was just asking him little questions," Gabriel says. "He wasn't cooperating. It's not my fault."

"You really shouldn't go around stabbing people, dude," Saint mutters.

Gabriel perks up. "And *you* shouldn't go around shooting people in the face. It's rude."

Saint stares at him.

"It was, uh, your reaction to Elora's death," Jace says. "You shot Kronos in the face a bunch of times."

"Then tried to drown yourself," Apollo adds.

That part probably wasn't necessary.

Saint considers that. "Huh. Sounds about right."

We're all doomed.

"So." I clap my newly freed hands together, drawing their attention away from Saint and his messed-up head. "Tem has a plan to un-fuck this city?"

31 REESE

I KEEP my back to the wall and my gaze on Gabriel. I do not trust the asshole, even though his zip ties have been replaced with metal handcuffs and he has Apollo and Jace like armed guards on either side of him. Saint hovers next to me, and he keeps glancing my way like he's worried I might explode.

Honestly? I've been considering it.

"Have you spoken to your friend?" Saint asks under his breath.

Currently, Jace and Kade are arguing about Olympus. It's a weird discussion—Jace thinks it would be good to reclaim that space and use it as our home base. Kade's pointing out how easy it was for Ouranos to wipe out the Hell Hounds' clubhouse because they were all in one centralized location.

But, we're in a centralized location *here*, and it's a lot less secure. Hidden, yes. The only way we've remained safe is because Ouranos and the Cyclopes haven't known where to look for us. Everything else in Sterling Falls is under scrutiny. This little house, with its long, nondescript driveway that makes it invisible from the road, is gold.

And we need to continue to keep it safe by not drawing attention to it. The moment we mobilize, the potential of outing ourselves increases. Even tire marks in the snow could be suspicious.

"I haven't wanted to..." I shrug.

"Did you know she's from Sterling Falls?"

"We used to talk." I wince. "Her partner got involved with the Cyclopes. Drugs, gambling. The coward fled, and Ouranos took Elodie in as payment. It wasn't Terror, but she wasn't free to leave. She was the entertainment for the lower-level guys, so I saw her around. It took a while before I realized it wasn't consensual on her part."

"Shit." Saint exhales. "But when he moved his operation up here, she remained?"

"He sold her to the gang leader in Emerald Cove as some show of... I don't fucking know. All I know is that I couldn't do anything as a teenager to stop the abuse in Terror—but I protected her as long as I could when I was there. And then she was gone."

Saint claps his hand on my shoulder. "You freed her from that shit."

"Too little, too late. Why couldn't I have gotten her out sooner? Why didn't I just open the door and let her run?" The guilt eats at me. In my mind, I had a mission to absolve myself, and it didn't include Elodie.

Dumb idiot.

Then, when I realized I *could* free her—that I needed to move on to Sterling Falls immediately, because Ouranos was closer than ever to enacting his plan—she was already gone.

Sold.

The feeling of stepping into the club and expecting to see her, the nervous excitement that I was going to be able to take her out of there, quickly turned to dread when it was a new face that greeted me.

"You should go," Saint urges. "She's upstairs."

I grimace. "I will. But not right now."

"Olympus is defendable," Jace says. "It's on a freaking cliffside, and the surrounding area is cleared out. There's no way for someone to sneak up on us there."

"So when Wolfe's father took it over, it was because you let it happen?" Daniel asks. "I'm sorry, but I remember hiding out at Tem's club coming up with plans to disrupt the war. Olympus was already gone."

"Bow & Arrow is out of the question," Artemis says. "Ouranos wants to bring Terror back, and my club stands above it."

Gabriel twists his fingers together. "Perhaps that is where the trap shall be laid, hmm?"

She goes still.

"He wants Terror, but he doesn't know the meaning of the word." Gabriel leans forward. "I think he likes the stench of others' fear. It's why being a judge wasn't enough. He wanted to be judge, jury, and executioner. He's never had a reason to be afraid, himself. He's never felt the cold sweat on his brow, the prickle of horror sliding down his spine. He doesn't know Terror like we do, sweet Artemis, but we could show him."

Slowly, she nods.

I close my eyes.

"It's decided, then." Her voice is a lot surer than I could've guessed. "We're going back to Terror."

32 ARTEMIS

REESE. Saint. Kade. Jace. Apollo. Gabriel. *Me.*

Daniel is in our ears, tapped into CCTV around the city. He's at home with Kora, Wolfe, Antonio, Vittoria, and the recluse. Wolfe is armed, Daniel is on guard, and the boat is ready to go in case they need to evacuate.

I grip my gun tighter. There's a lot at stake here, and the first step is exterminating the vermin currently infesting my home.

North Falls feels different without a nightlife. There are no tourists. The restaurants that line the boardwalk are shut down, and my beloved club is silent. At this time of year, with winter roaring through the town, there wouldn't be that many tourists anyway. But there would still be a buzz of life that is absent at the moment.

We ditched our vehicles blocks away. It was easier to avoid the roadblocks by cutting through alleys and clinging to the shadows.

Gabriel stands to my left. His spine is straight, and

his hands are still cuffed. Reese stands directly behind him, one hand on his shoulder and a gun jammed into his lower back.

Overkill, I want to say, but my voice stopped working some time ago.

Before we left, Antonio reminded us of the second tunnel to get into Terror. So that's our plan—we're taking the back way in to my club. My bravado was a *lot* stronger back in the safety of my brother's home.

"You really did put lipstick on a pig," Gabriel says.

I glance at him.

He gestures with both hands to the building. "It's like building an amusement park on stilts on top of an active volcano."

"Say what you really mean," I mumble.

"It's like running a cat sanctuary when you're deathly allergic," he continues. "Or trying to get a hair out of your eye with a knife. Or playing a million-dollar violin with a chainsaw. Or—"

"She gets it." Reese jabs the gun into the small of his back.

Gabriel twists around. "I was hoping you would be here."

I roll my eyes.

"All clear," Daniel says in our ears.

"Move," Jace orders.

"Kade isn't in handcuffs," Gabriel observes. "And I am?"

"You're a bit more murderous," Reese grunts. "And a wild card."

He shoves him forward, keeping up with the force of men in front of us. We're at the tail end of our little pack. Everyone else is single file: Jace then Apollo, Saint, Kade. Then me, Gabriel, and Reese.

Speaking of cards—there's a trump card in my back pocket that I haven't revealed yet. I'm holding that as a *just in case*. Gabriel hasn't asked about Lyssa, which makes me think he's unaware of the bomb Reese set off, or the disruption to the entire island. Yes, he made some claims about not being able to go to her. His urgency seemed... lacking.

As far as everyone on Isle of Paradise knows, save Dr. Hawthorne, she's been transferred off the island.

Does he know she's awake? Probably not.

Does he think she's been moved? Definitely not.

His freak-out would be much more severe.

That is the card Ouranos will play. We can't be trusted because we stole Lyssa. Only he can help Gabriel find her.

I grit my teeth. We enter the darkened alley, the street now at our backs still empty. It's been quiet, which is good. It feels wrong, but it's a good thing. We cut through the darkness like a surgeon's blade, quick and efficient.

Gabriel even keeps his mouth shut.

Jace gets to the door and positions himself just to the side. Apollo wraps his hand around the handle and waits for Jace's signal.

The door opens with a sharp squeal, and Jace enters in a rush. The rest of us follow, flooding the hallway. We click on our flashlights. I feel Gabriel's fingers grasping at the back of my jacket as we move along.

Apollo is now at the back of the pack. He closes the door behind us and moves to catch up.

"All good?" he asks me.

I nod once. He checks in with Reese, but his gaze lingers on Gabriel.

Gabriel has gone very, very still. Yes, his legs still move. He is propelled forward by Reese. But the rest of his body is all locked up.

"You've been down here plenty of times," I say.

"Yes, yes." He shakes his head hard. "Just old memories, sweet Artemis. You know."

I bite the inside of my cheek. I *would* know if I let myself think on it. But I don't. Apollo squeezes my forearm.

"Wonder if those files have donor information," Reese muses.

Gabriel cranes back. "What?"

"There are files on everyone who went through Terror," Apollo explains. "We have them. We haven't gone through everything—"

"So there could be some sort of... blackmail," Reese finishes.

"No one cares." I quicken my pace. "No one gives a damn about Terror. It existed under everyone's noses for years. That's why..."

"I tried to blow it up," Gabriel says. "I was stopped."

"Because the nightclub above it was full of innocent people," Reese says.

Right. That was just at the beginning, wasn't it? When Gabriel fought at Olympus and promised ruin, when Kade asked for the day with me to get my help with locating Reese...

"You weren't trying to destroy Terror. You were sending me a message." I push my shoulders back. This hallway has gone on forever, but we're nearly at the end. Then we'll truly be back in Terror.

One of the guys' flashlights sweeps back and shines in our faces.

"Enough," Kade says. "You won't solve anything right now. Focus."

He faces forward again, and I stick out my tongue at his back. He's right—I just don't like being told what to do. We're all dressed in pseudo-military gear that Jace pulled out of a locked cabinet in the basement. The Kevlar vest is strapped tight to my torso. My hair is in two braids. The comms are wired, threaded down the back of my shirt and into a tiny pack on the utility belt Wolfe tossed at me.

I wasn't ready for the pants Kora presented me with. Black canvas, with way more pockets than I was expecting. They're a little long, the hem rolled so I don't trip, and the hips are tight. Otherwise, they fit pretty well.

I also wasn't ready for the blisteringly hot look Kade gave me when I emerged in it, a tight long-sleeve black shirt, and the vest. I felt that look down to my toes. If we weren't in a room full of people, I had the impression that he would've been tempted to do something.

Like haul me in and kiss me senseless?

Focus, idiot.

I have a handgun in a holster at my hip. A knife with a wicked blade on my left side. Extra magazines tucked in every available pocket—*and there are a lot of pockets.*

The true beauty is the semi-automatic rifle that Wolfe handed to me. That weapon is currently in my hands, the flashlight attached to the top of it. Jace and Apollo have them, too, which left smaller firearms for Saint and Reese.

While Kade is free, he wasn't given a weapon.

Fine by me.

We reach the familiar, heavy door, but it's been left open. Jace goes first, as always, with Saint on his heel. Kade moves with him, his steps fluid. He's done this before, and the lack of weapon doesn't seem to cause any hitch in his gait. No hesitation.

Me next, then Gabriel, Reese, and Apollo. We collect together in the hallway, trading glances.

The emergency lights are on. They buzz overhead.

Gabriel flinches.

Without thinking, I reach across and put my hand over his balled fist. I squeeze gently, then move away. He needs to be okay for this part.

In all honesty, he probably could've stayed at the house. The risk of leaving him with Kora, Antonio, and Vittoria, though, outweighed the danger of bringing him with us. He's already gotten away with too much. What if he was tempted to do something... worse? To them?

Anyway. The plan is simple: we take control of Bow & Arrow. We don't know who is currently here, or what sort of traps they have rigged. We do know, thanks to Gabriel and Kade, that Ouranos has set up the Cyclopes here. They aren't sleeping here, as far as I know, but it's a meeting point.

Which means we could be walking into fifty Cyclopes or five.

Gabriel said Ouranos is still operating his meetings out of Madness, the bar in West Falls. It was his brother's bar—before it got caught in an explosion—so it makes sense that he'd want to be there. A bit of optimism.

Too bad the subway tunnels are all caved in, Apollo had said.

I smiled even though I also wanted to punch him. That damn subway car full of explosives nearly killed us. And while we were dealing with that, Saint was losing Nyx.

We stay in a loose formation until we reach the exit that will lead us up into the club. Gabriel withholds any other physical reaction, which is good. I don't know if I can deal with a breakdown. The walls already feel like they're closing in, the ceiling lowering.

Up, up, up. To the main level, then higher. To the offices on the top floor. My legs are tingling with fatigue by the time we reach our destination. I suck in a deep breath and motion that I'll take the lead. Yes, Jace and Apollo—and Saint, not that he freaking remembers—have been here plenty of times before. They know where my office is.

But... I need to see what they've done. I need to see it first.

Someone calls after me, but there's a rushing noise in my ears that muffles the sound. I'm in my own world as I creep down toward my office. The hallway is dark, which lends a certain level of comfort. There are no bright lights to expose us. Nothing coming from under my or Antonio's office doors.

Still, when I open mine—it's unlocked—my breath catches in my chest.

It's been ransacked. The desk is in pieces, chunks of splintered wood on the floor. The computer had been previously removed when Bradshaw raided it, and most of the paper files were in Antonio's... but that doesn't mean it's not jarring. There's glass mixed in amongst the wood, the few framed photos and art on the walls knocked down and ruined.

Even chunks of drywall have been kicked in.

Unnecessary. The safe is built into the floor of Antonio's office. Which might be in danger judging by the level of destruction.

Apollo comes up behind me and sucks in a sharp breath. "Sorry, Tem."

I shake my head and turn away. "We'll fix it. When we take back this city. It's all things that can be repaired."

He grabs my hand. "So long as we don't lose anyone else who we love."

I wish I could say the lump that closes my throat is unexpected.

33 SAINT

BOW & Arrow is different. It might be that the overhead light's on, and the glamour that Tem managed to craft in this building has been peeled away. But it seems like more than that. There's a darkness here that seeps up from Terror. It's the shadow that tracks us down the hallways.

I feel it in the stiffness of Tem's shoulders. She's in front of us now, her body tense. I want to go up and shield her from this, because this club...

We pass her office, and Kade and I peer inside.

I wince. *Poor Tem.* I imagine discovering Starlight, my tattoo shop, destroyed like this, and can sympathize with the emotions she must be grappling with.

Kade nudges me onward.

We sweep through the kitchen, and Jace motions for two of us to go check the large, rooftop restaurant space. Apollo and Kade go. We wait for a long moment, handfuls of seconds, before they return with a quick, muttered, "Clear."

The rest of us follow them back out, cutting through the restaurant to get to the staircase that will lead us down into the club.

This is arguably the riskiest part. The staircase is against the wall, but one side is made of glass. It allows patrons an unfiltered look into the club below, especially for the late-night dining guests passing through on their way up.

I move forward, to where Artemis stands next to her brother, and catch her wrist.

She jumps.

"Let us go first," I say.

"Us?"

"Us," Kade replies at my shoulder. "Or, at the very least, me. They won't react when they see me. They'll expect me here. I can take them out."

Gabriel cracks his neck. "Sounds juicy. Can I come, too?"

I had forgotten that twisted fucker was here.

He holds out his cuffed hands. "I don't need a gun. A knife will suffice."

"So you can stab Kade in the back?" Jace snaps.

Gabriel eyes him. "No, Hades. I got in the car with them, didn't I? I'm on your side."

For now.

Also, he's leaving out the part where he kind of made a scene after agreeing to come with us and we forcibly *put* him in the trunk. I don't think I've ever seen Artemis madder than when he tried to run. She *tackled* him.

It was probably cathartic.

They wrestled on the ground, and she managed to pin his arms at his sides, straddling his body.

Hot.

Too hot.

Don't-think-about-it-right-now hot.

Then she said she had zip ties in the trunk, and her expression turned sly. It was easy enough to know where she was going with that. Gabriel, meet trunk. He took it pretty well, and I thought he'd come out a bit more vicious. If anything, Tem's insane driving on the way back settled him.

Jace squints at Gabriel, perhaps trying to take his stock, but the dude is unstable. There's no telling if this offer will end up being a double-cross... or worse.

"I'm fine with it," Kade says. "We're on the same side, Gabe and I."

"Don't call me that." He runs his fingers through his hair. "How do I look? Dashing? Heroic?"

"Sure," Kade agrees.

Apollo shakes his head and slowly removes the knife from his boot. He hands it to Gabriel, and Jace gives Kade a handgun.

"Don't fuck us over," Reese mutters.

Kade looks at him, his brows pinching together. "We're done with that."

Reese doesn't seem convinced, but he doesn't say anything else.

"Oh!" Gabriel brightens. "I think someone you know is here."

We all stop and stare at him.

"Who?" Tem finally asks.

Gabriel makes some vague motion. "Terrible man. He was most unforthcoming. Surprising survival instinct, though. The boss didn't want me to kill him. Had a doctor out, even, once they dragged him in."

"*Who?*"

"The Hell Hounds' leader." He sighs. "Don't make me remember his name. I only recall the way he wheezed after his lungs were punctured."

Ah, for fuck's sake.

I grab Artemis when she's mid-lunge. Her feet leave the floor, her weight suddenly fully in my grasp. Momentum carries her forward. Her fingers come within an inch of his face. Kade shoves Gabriel back. I swing her around, too aware of the feel of her body on mine. She struggles against me. Her face reddens.

"Easy." I put my hand on her face.

Why am I touching her face?

"Calm down."

Her gaze darts to mine. "Calm *down?* You must have learned better than to say that—"

"We are in a precarious situation, and you freaking the fuck out will not help." I band my free arm tighter around her, but my palm on her cheek is unbearably gentle. "So, yeah, calm down and deal with the emotions on the other side of this."

"Go," Jace says to Kade and Gabriel.

I keep Tem's attention on me. I want her eyes. I want her focus.

I want her scowling, smiling, insulting...

We've been in this position before. Locked together. Angry.

Except this time, it's not me who's furious.

"He could've told us before," she says. "We could've made a plan to get Malik out—"

"*If* he's here," I reason. "They could've brought him to the hospital. He doesn't sound sure."

Pain flashes across her face, and she finally goes still. She grasps my wrist and squeezes. "I just can't watch anyone else..."

I shake my head fast. I've been dreaming a lot about blood lately... and I think it's Elora's. I think I'm beginning to remember pieces of her death. The agony of watching her die... No, I don't want to live through something like that again. I care about everyone here, minus one torturing lunatic.

How would we survive another loss?

A gunshot cracks in the distance. We reflexively drop into crouches.

There's another, followed by a shout. I eye my brother, who shifts ever so slightly in front of me. I can't find it in me to be mad—he's always had a protective streak.

The overhead lights flicker, then go out. We're doused in darkness for a long moment, still and silent, before we click on our flashlights again. With a twist on the top, we switch them over to a red-light mode.

"Shit," Jace mutters. "Okay, we're splitting up. Saint and Reese, come with me. Apollo and Artemis, go back the way we came and clear us an exit in case things get dicey."

We all nod, our faces barely visible in the collective red glow. I don't particularly want to leave Artemis—a weird gut reaction—but she turns and follows her brother back the way we came, sticking to the wall and moving fast. She doesn't look back.

Reese elbows me, and I adjust my grip on my weapon. There's another volley of gunshots, these higher-pitched. A different caliber of gun, the *pop-pop-pop* familiar and alarming at the same time.

I grimace. Reese opens the door for Jace and me. We move fast, and I take a little comfort in the idea that Reese has professional training. Not that I love the idea of him going to war, but he seems unbothered that we're in the middle of another one.

We hurry down and pause on a landing that splits into the upper, VIP level of the club. Jace glances down it, frowning, then points to Reese.

I swallow when Reese moves silently down the hall on his own.

Jace points at me and then down the stairs.

Onward.

We descend into the belly of the club. Kade and Gabriel are probably ahead of us somewhere, but the club was made to hold shadows and secrets. Part of its charm, Tem would say. With the low strobe lights and wall sconces, the whole vibe is dark luxury.

Right now, it's just plain dark.

The hallways twist. There are semi-private rooms and areas all over the place. Balconies with glass walls look down onto the main dance floor, the VIP sections Reese is clearing and spaces for the average client.

There are suspended platforms for dancers, too, meant to hover out in the open.

I glance up, aware that anyone could be hiding in those upper rooms and spot us. The platforms aren't visible. Everything is... black.

Pop-pop-pop

I catch up to Jace and put my hand on his shoulder. We continue, and it isn't until we reach one of the bars that we find our first body. My chest tightens until Jace's light sweeps over the face.

Not Kade.

It's not Gabriel either, but the clean bullet hole in the center of the guy's forehead suggests it's Kade's kill.

Someone emerges ahead of us, and Jace registers that it's a Cyclops before I can raise my gun. He fires twice. The man jerks as he falls, his gun going off and putting bullets into the wall to our left.

Jace moves forward and finishes the kill, and I shake off my nerves. We find more bodies along the way, then come to a fork.

"Take the right," he says. "Shoot first, ask questions later."

Right. Minus the whole not-shooting-one-of-us thing.

We separate, and the corridor I'm in leads back to the dance floor. I come out near the silent, barren DJ platform. There's a *bang* to my left, and I spin around, my red light arcing across the empty space.

Nothing.

I'm fucking jumpy. I'm not built for this.

Something hums—electricity, maybe—and then the lights overhead flicker back to life. I squint and quickly scan the area, but it's empty.

"Hey!" someone shouts.

I whirl, just in time to catch a glimpse of Gabriel rushing at me with something over his head. He swings it, his handcuffs glinting, and nails me in the side of the head.

I see stars, then nothing at all.

34 ARTEMIS

APOLLO and I get five Cyclopes in the stairwell. I'm not sure if they intended on circling around to pin us in—I don't think it ever got to that point. But eventually, we run into Kade who smirks at me and gives us a thumbs-up. He's got a bit of blood smeared across his forehead and dusted on his Kevlar vest.

"There were no leaders," he explains. "It was being used as a hang-out spot, but that's it. We caught it at a good time."

Right. We get the power back on—Kade and Gabriel were the ones who killed it in the first place—and head back toward the main level. Saint, Jace, and Reese should be around here somewhere.

"Where is Gabriel, by the way?" Apollo asks. He peers over his shoulder, then makes a face at me. "Shouldn't he be with you?"

"Should be," Kade grunts. "He slipped away. I assume one of the others will find him soon enough."

Famous last words. I exchange another look with my brother.

"There you guys are," Reese calls, coming down one of the staircases that leads to VIP. "Where's Jace? Saint?"

"Haven't found them yet," Kade says.

"And Gabriel is MIA," I add.

Reese scowls.

"Was there anyone in VIP?" Apollo asks.

"Two. They were drunk, don't even think they knew there was trouble till I shot the first one."

Oye.

We make it to the dance floor, which is empty except for a body.

Not a body.

Saint.

Saint is on the floor, curled on his side, and he's not moving.

"Oh God." I shove my gun into my brother's chest and rush across the dance floor, falling to my knees at his side. "Please be alive. Please be alive."

I push his shoulder and roll him onto his back. It takes me a second to rip through the Velcro of his vest and get access to his chest. I pat him down, feeling for blood, for any wetness, but there's nothing. There *is* blood on his temple, nearly blending in with his dark hair.

"*Saint,*" I choke out. I put my fingers to his throat and pray for a pulse.

I hardly believe it when I feel it.

He lets out a low groan, his brows furrowing. He opens his eyes slowly, blinking rapidly.

I lean over him, torn between shaking him for scaring me and—

His blue eyes lock on to my face, and he smiles.

Smiles?

"Tem," he breathes.

Something in the way he says it makes my throat close.

He touches my cheek, but he doesn't seem all here. His arm falls to the floor, his body going limp. His eyes roll back, and he passes out again.

35 SAINT

I REMEMBER EVERYTHING.

36 ARTEMIS

WE MOVE SAINT—OKAY, Reese and Kade move Saint—up to one of the VIP sections. The whole way up, I have flashbacks to Jace and Wolfe carrying in Nyx. We brought her here after she died, covered her in a sheet... It was traumatic. We were all watching Saint like he was made of glass, waiting for him to shatter.

Apollo and I had missed it. Her death, I mean. We'd missed it because we were off in another part of Sterling Falls, investigating the closed, abandoned subway tunnels. And nearly getting blown up in the process.

I thought *we* had it rough, and then the ground dropped out from below me when I learned about my best friend.

I brush a tear away, and Reese looks over at me. When they've set down Saint, he approaches and wraps his arms around me. I sink into his hug and exhale roughly. His scent, the cedar and smoke I'm so familiar with, is buried under gunpowder. But it's still there.

He didn't used to smell like that. In Terror, he had a different aftershave. His taste has refined... or he wanted to separate his current self from the boy who was forced to participate.

"You okay?" he asks the top of my head.

"Getting there."

After another minute, I straighten. I unstrap my Kevlar vest and remove the rest of the weapons, setting everything down on another table. I take inventory of the ammo I used, the magazine and a half left remaining. The longer I fiddle with everything, the less my hands shake.

Jace comes over and sits across from me. He watches me silently, but I *feel* his quiet judgment. I'm the one who brought Gabriel back, after all. I'm the one who thought he could be redeemed.

"What?" I finally ask.

"Sit down, Tem, your legs are about to give out."

I glare at him, then follow the order. I lean back in the booth and take a deep breath. Then another. My pulse is fast and fluttery.

Someone nudges me deeper into the booth, and I move automatically. I don't bother opening—I assume it's Reese or Apollo. Either would be a welcome comfort.

"Artemis." It's Kade's voice beside me. The low rumble. "Drink this."

I squint at the table. The tall glass filled with ice and a clear liquid. It's either liquor or water, and I don't suppose either would taste bad at this moment. Even so, it takes a second for my limbs to move, for my arm to lift and stretch across the table. Longer still for the cold condensation to register against my fingertips.

"Hey," Apollo says.

I glance over, but his phone is pressed to his ear.

"Yeah, we're all clear here. Are the comms not working?" He focuses on Jace. "Might be a jammer somewhere. We didn't notice."

I forgot about them. I pull the earbud out and drop it on the table. I think I was a little distracted... Okay, a lot distracted. The fact that Daniel completely cut out and I didn't realize is... concerning.

"I'll go take a look around. Tell him to keep an eye out on the street." Jace slides out and stands, then pauses and glances down at me.

"We should put the bodies out front," Kade says casually.

Jace narrows his eyes.

"As a warning that it's no longer a safe space for the Cyclopes." Kade tips his head. "I can help with that."

"It's a good idea," Apollo says, shocking the hell out of me. "Tem can stay with Saint while we do the heavy lifting."

Reese, seated on a bar stool across from us, grimaces and hops to his feet.

In a flurry, they all leave.

I'm left holding my glass of... water? Vodka?

I pick it up and sniff it, then take a sip. Cold water coats my tongue, and I nearly groan. I chug half of it before I gain some self-control and set it down.

Sitting still is out of the question.

I check on Saint. I take his pulse again, my fingers at his wrist this time. Put my hand to his forehead. Inspect the wound at his temple. It's stopped bleeding, which is the best case scenario.

"Okay," I say under my breath. "Now what?"

I stare around at the VIP section. The glass walls, the U-shaped booths, the bar.

It's actually a disaster zone. There's blood on the floor, along with garbage, bits of glass littered everywhere. The bigger pieces are visible up against the footwell of the bar and along the walls, out of the way, but still a problem.

For fuck's sake.

So I start cleaning. There's a closet just outside the section, the door a hidden panel that blends quite nicely into the wall. It's invisible when the club is open, the darkness obscuring all my little tricks. I gather supplies and head back, starting first by sweeping everything into a pile. There are some sticky sections, probably from spilled drinks, that I ignore until I can get to the mop.

I'm on my third pass with the broom—and hopefully the last—when Saint wakes up.

I drop it and rush to his side. "You're back with us."

He touches his temple and frowns. "Freaking Gabriel cold-cocked me."

"Yeah."

He sits up slowly, looking around, and swings his legs over the edge. His feet make indents in the booth cushions, and he takes a moment with his elbows on his thighs.

"Water?" I scramble around the bar and find a clean glass. That alone seems like a miracle. I rinse it out then fill it and bring it back.

"Thanks." He accepts it and drinks deeply, his throat bobbing with every swallow. When it's gone, he hands it back.

I don't know what to do, so I just hold it and stare.

How on earth do I tell him that the thought of him dying is one of my most terrifying?

"Tem..." He winces and reaches for my free hand. "I'm so sorry."

I blink. "For what?"

"For everything that's happened since you came to my hospital room after the car accident." He squeezes my fingers, his blue eyes burning. "For telling you I loved you and then treating you like I hated you."

Wait—what?

He remembers that?

My mouth opens and shuts, but I can't seem to get any words out.

"For tattooing Kade when I knew it would hurt you," he continues. "For not seeing that you were screaming in agony for weeks after what Gabriel did. For our first time having sex being as rough and as cruel as I was. Oh—don't cry."

I'm not, I want to say, but then he reaches up and swipes my cheek, smearing wetness across my skin.

"Elora has always been the stars," he says softly. "But you're the goddamn sun. And I'm sorry I ever made you feel like you weren't."

He takes the glass from my hand and sets it aside, then tows me in.

When his lips meet mine, it's not hard. It's not demanding.

It's so sweet, it makes me want to sob. I inch closer, but there's too much in the way. The way he's seated, the side of the booth, the table. He makes a noise in the back of his throat, a sound of frustration, and suddenly grabs me by the hips and lifts me. I get my knee on the table and swing my other over him, settling on his lap straddling him. I immediately wrap my arms around his shoulders. My nails drift under the collar of his shirt and up his neck.

He hums, deepening the kiss. He tugs my braid to angle my head the way he wants it.

He remembers.

The pain of the last few weeks doesn't go away, but this certainly helps.

I need to be closer.

I slide my palms down the center of his chest and go for his pants. His tongue sweeps into my mouth, and it's all I can do to stay focused on the task. Once his dick is out, I wrap my fingers around it, squeezing and moving my palm up and down. He's hard, but it stiffens further in my grasp.

"Your pants," he says against my lips.

I undo the button and shove them down. I use his shoulder for balance and stand on the booth seat, between his legs, and get them down to my ankles. Before I can get back into position, he holds my hips and leans forward. His breath coasts along my pubic bone. He kisses there, then lower. I lean back and widen my stance for him to give my clit attention. He pushes a finger into me and hums in appreciation.

I'm already on the verge of losing it, and he's barely touched me.

"Come here." He finally withdraws, and he smirks at my expression. "Hmm, I remember that look."

"Good," I breathe.

I straddle him again, and his hand slips between my legs. He brings me to the edge, his gaze glued to my face.

"So responsive," he murmurs. "When's the last time you came, wildcat?"

I whimper. I truly didn't think I'd ever hear him call me that again.

"Words," he admonishes.

Same old Saint.

My pussy clenches. *It is the same old Saint.* Resurrected.

"It's been a few weeks..."

He tsks. "No one's been touching you?"

"Been a little busy," I grit out. "You've been sharing a room with Reese—"

"Hmm. You can share it with us."

Oh, fuck.

That edge? He catapults me off it. I come with his fingers inside me and his thumb on my clit. I arch my back, my vision going white. Pleasure radiates through me. I barely notice his withdrawal, but when his cock inches into me, I gasp. My orgasm seems to be rolling on, his attention on my clit never wavering. Even as he lowers me onto him.

It's sensation overload.

He grips the back of my neck with one hand, guiding my movement. Up, down. The friction, the stretch—it's too much. His lips brush my throat. Then his teeth.

I take over the motion, rolling my hips and finding the sweet spot. My legs tremble every time he hits it, but I can't stop. I chase the feeling, my eyes shut tight.

Am I dreaming?

Maybe Gabriel hit *my* head. I'm the one lying on a table unconscious right now, having sex dreams about Saint Hart.

"Look at me," Saint growls.

I force myself to open my eyes and focus on him. It's then that I come. It sneaks up on me, but his grip on my neck tightens. It's a silent reminder not to close him out—close my eyes—again. And I don't.

I let myself feel everything I can for this man before fate decides to steal it away again.

37 KADE

REESE, Jace, Apollo, and I are almost back to the VIP room when the sounds of sex stop us. Reese looks from Jace to Apollo, his eyes crinkling with his smile.

"Maybe you guys should get back to your house. Check on Kora and Wolfe," he suggests. "Clear out for a few hours..."

Jace huffs, seemingly caught between amused and disgusted. Apollo, though, is firmly in the *disgusted* camp. He grabs Jace and hauls him back the way we came.

I snicker at their hasty exit, then focus on Reese.

"What?" I question.

"I'm just..." Reese sighs. "I don't know what to think about you."

I sober. "That's understandable."

"Do we trust you? After everything—"

"Yes," I say simply. "I regret the decisions I made that led us to here. And I will spend however long it takes apologizing for them."

The truth of the matter is, I thought Ouranos was right. In the beginning anyway. He was a means to an end when I first arrived, and then I got sucked in and lost my moral compass. *Clearly*, I couldn't see what was right in front of my face: that his takeover of Sterling Falls would result in a lot of deaths.

I believed him when he said it would be peaceful and that the things he was setting into motion were for a gentle takeover.

Then he set a rabid dog—*Gabriel*—loose.

"Okay," Reese says. "Artemis is the final judgment call on that, man. But it means a lot for me to hear you say that."

I smile just as the sounds of Tem's climax reaches us.

Damn, that's hot.

Without another word, Reese and I enter the room. I'm not sure exactly what I pictured, but Tem straddling Saint, with his hand on the back of her neck and their intense eye contact, was not it. They're not kissing, but her hips move slowly. They don't notice us—they're locked in an intimate moment, which is the first I've seen of them in a while.

And they're fully clothed except for where they're joined... which just won't do.

Anticipation prickles at my skin, but I hesitate. After everything, I don't know if my touch is welcome. Reese strides forward, but I hang back. He makes a comment that has Artemis focusing on him, and her lazy smile creates a knot of tension in my chest.

He kisses her.

"Kade," Saint rumbles.

I focus on him, and shock flickers through me. He seems different. He's the version of Saint Hart that I expected to find on Isle of Paradise. Cocky, self-assured. Aware of our history and not afraid of it.

"You remember?"

He nods. He doesn't seem to mind that Reese and Artemis are now making out while he's still inside her. He just leans back, giving them room, and inclines his chin.

A dare.

I take a step forward. Then another.

"Saint, I—"

"Save it for later," he says. His body flexes, hips thrusting his cock into Tem, and she moans into Reese's mouth. "Come here."

I approach. I stop at the edge of the table. Reese has a knee on the seat and a hand planted next to Tem's thigh. I stare at them, at their tongues, and my heart skips.

She breaks away and focuses on me. Her gaze sharpens.

Here comes the part where she tells me to get lost. She reaches out and curls her fingers around the top edge of my vest. Instead of shoving me away, she drags me in. I catch myself on the table and lean in.

She kisses me.

She's kissing me.

Why is she kissing me?

Every warm feeling about her, that I've been trying to bury for weeks, suddenly rushes to the surface. I didn't want to become attached. I didn't want to think about her at night. I didn't want to betray her to save Reese.

My heart cracks open at all I put her through.

All I put *them* through. Saint and Tem and Reese—they've been a unit, and I've been their opposition.

Why?

Fucking *why?*

I pull away and shake my head, but she still has a hold on my vest. She hangs on, not allowing me to get far.

"I'm sorry," I blurt out. Saint said to save it, but I can't contain myself. "I'm so fucking sorry, Artemis."

She exhales.

"You're in a burning building," Reese says suddenly. "Who are you saving?"

I meet Tem's eyes. "You."

Her brows furrow.

"You're in a burning building," Reese says again, but this time, he's staring at Saint. "Who are you saving?"

"We've already had this conversation," Saint says.

He grasps Tem's hips and lifts her off him. Reese helps her stand, and he pulls her pants up. His tattooed cock stands at attention, the head an angry red color. It's the only part that isn't covered in ink. The length of him is wet from Tem's pussy.

Reese jerks. "You—"

"I'd dive back into it for any of you," he finishes.

"This is a hypothetical, though," Artemis says slowly. She buttons her pants and frowns. "And no one asked who I would save."

"You'd save all of us," I say.

"You already have," Reese adds.

She smiles.

It feels like a moment that should be underlined and saved

"Poor Saint," I murmur, focusing back on him. "You didn't come?"

He hasn't moved, but now he swings his legs around. I step out of the way and allow him the space to hop to his feet. He drags his jeans back up over his boner, somehow managing to get the zipper up and the button done.

"Time for that later," he says.

Artemis looks ready to argue, but he shakes his head.

"No. Let's deal with our problems so it isn't hanging over us."

He has a point.

"Ouranos," Reese says. "And the Cyclopes."

Artemis sighs and rubs her eyes. "Bradshaw is in the hospital... but do we know where Malik is? Didn't Gabriel say he might be here? I can't believe I forgot—"

"You were a bit distracted," Reese murmurs.

I frown. "He wasn't in the building. We cleared the whole thing."

Saint grabs her hand and kisses her knuckles. "We'll find him."

"He's like family," she says to me and Reese. "I grew up..."

"You were in the Hell Hounds?" I ask. That's news to me.

"No." She climbs down from the seat and slips

between us. On the other table are her weapons that she unloaded earlier. "No, I didn't. Apollo, Jace, and Wolfe did, and I was... around. Where else would I have gone? Malik was always like a brother to them. An older, annoying brother. He taught them the ropes. And, by default, I was the annoying little sister tagging along when Cerberus wasn't looking."

Saint snorts.

"From Terror to the Hell Hounds..." Reese seems stricken. "And you can still smile?"

"I'm sure you saw worse." She peeks over her shoulder at us. "You were deployed. You saw real war. You smile just fine."

"He didn't for a while, Tem," I tell her.

"The military was penance." Reese elbows me. "It's fine."

"You know what *isn't* fine?" Tem turns around.

The handgun is back in its holster at her hip, the wide belt accenting her figure. The Kevlar vest is strapped on tight, and she holds the rifle her brother gave her. I'm sure the rest of her magazines are in pockets, a knife in her boot... Everything about her screams *warrior*. But she's not, is she? She's a martyr for this city. She'd rather die for it than see it ruined.

Hell, she proved that by coming back here. By enduring everything she's been through.

She flicks her braid over her shoulder. "People come into this city with *plans*. They keep trying to take what's ours. But it isn't for sale. It's not up for grabs. And we don't go down without a fight."

Reese sucks in a breath. One look at his face tells me everything: he's invested.

He didn't answer his own question—about the burning building—but I have no doubt he would run through Hell to save Artemis.

Tem lifts her chin. "Lucky for you guys, I have a plan."

LISTENING to Artemis talk soothes something inside me. She's smart and articulate. Those are traits I *knew* she possessed, but I absolutely appreciate and admire them. She sees the big picture and paints the picture for us.

Ouranos is the queen bee, and the Cyclopes are his soldiers. Kade confirms that beyond himself and Gabriel, there aren't true leaders within their ranks. It isn't like the military. They're given orders at random, paired together as it suits Ouranos. They're just pawns moved across the board, sacrificed at will.

And, like a true cult leader, Ouranos has convinced all of them that his will can lead them to some sort of salvation. He used that tactic on Kade, didn't he? Maybe with a more personal touch... maybe with a bit more manipulation. But the messaging is the same, and it's widespread. Surround yourself with like-minded people, become a mass or a horde or a swarm, and you'll forget the individual.

They might've had objections, but there is nowhere to voice them. Ouranos perfected a combination of fear and adoration in his leadership.

And yet, at the heart of it, he is still Justice Marcus Graves of Emerald Cove. He's still a man. He was once four years old. He was once sixteen and acne-prone.

What he won't become is old, because his time is coming to an abrupt end.

Artemis has hinted at her plan for that, but what she's decided to focus on is the worker bees.

The Cyclopes.

We took out their meeting spot—here. We killed some and piled them on the sidewalk out front as a warning. We turned on the Bow & Arrow neon logo above the door.

It isn't much, but it kind of felt like a signal of a turning tide.

We didn't find that many here, but Artemis has determined a few reasons:

One, it might not have been a night where Ouranos had anything major planned. We struck on a whim, and in a way, we got lucky that there weren't more.

Two, the Cyclopes are in charge of enforcing a curfew across the city. I agree that it probably takes more manpower than we anticipated.

Three, they also have control of the sheriff's office. To suspect that they might *also* be holding that building would be logical.

Ouranos wanted Bow & Arrow for what's underneath. But strategically speaking, the center of town would give him a better vantage point. He would be able to dispatch the Cyclopes to all parts of the city faster, especially North and East Falls. They took West Falls early. North Falls isn't residential enough to cause a problem, especially once the club was theirs.

"Are you sure about this?" I call to Artemis.

She, Kade, and Saint are on motorcycles.

I'm in my truck, which has been packed to the nines with weapons. I am a driving arsenal... and I don't even have a backseat.

She winks at me, then slaps the tinted visor down over her helmet. Her bike is all black, and she sits astride it like she was born there. I have no idea where she procured it, along with Kade's and Saint's. I got back from retrieving my truck, and there they were.

The plan is to ride through town, cause a ruckus, and get the Cyclopes to chase them.

The sub-plan is to not get shot in the process.

She drew paths on a paper map for us. My eyes bugged out when she pulled that from a random drawer in the apartment. It sits on the seat beside me, held down by two boxes of ammo and another rifle.

There's a circled spot on the map where I need to meet them, and I should have about fifteen minutes to set up before they arrive—if it goes smoothly.

While they cause chaos, I'm going to head straight there. Apparently, as the only one who doesn't have a lot of bike experience, I got vetoed from the chaos squad.

Instead, since I *do* have experience with bombs... amongst other things... I got delegated this job.

I shake my head and climb out of the truck. I make a beeline for Artemis and gesture for her to take off her helmet. She does, her dark hair ruffled. She squints at me, confused, until I catch her face and slam my lips against hers.

This isn't really a *goodbye* kiss, but it damn sure is a *stay safe* kiss. I lick at the seam of her mouth. Her lips part, and I take a taste of her that will have to last me until we get back.

Because we're all going to get back in one piece.

She finally pushes me away with a smile and a shake of her head. She touches her lips, then puts her helmet back on.

I grin.

"See you on the other side," I call to them.

I follow the main road in North Falls west. I drive slow, my headlights off, and coast to a stop whenever I see another car. I avoid detection past the house Kade rented, past the dunes that mark the northwest edge of the town. From there, the road curves south. The forest on my right is thick and dark. To my left is West Falls, but there are no visible houses from here.

Artemis explained this road is used mainly as an access road for delivery trucks to get easily from the harbor in South Falls up to the businesses along the boardwalk. There's a turn-off for the reservoir on my right, and a driveway that leads up through the trees to an old, abandoned church. Or something. She was fuzzy on those details—not that it matters.

Saint seemed uncomfortable at the mention of that, too.

I pass those and check the map. I compare it to the map on my phone and nod to myself. My nerves are wreaking havoc, but I take a deep inhale and blow it out long and slow.

It's going to be fine.

I park and kill the engine. The windows have been down, just in case, and the faint sound of another engine pricks at my ears.

I sit perfectly still, straining to hear.

It gets louder.

Half a mile down the road, a truck slows to a stop at the intersection of this road and theirs. Their headlights shine onto the trees across the road, everything about the vehicle meant to be loud and abrasive.

"Don't turn this way," I mumble. I fold up the map and shove it in my back pocket, then quickly strap on the rifle. I drop the ammunition into the small space behind the passenger seat and haul out an old blanket. With as small movement as possible, I cover the boxes on the floor of the cab.

The truck turns in my direction.

"Shit." I slide across the bench seat and crack the passenger door. I hop out and close it as quietly as possible, crouch-running into the woods in the darkness. I have no idea if anyone saw me, but I keep going, scrambling uphill until I can only barely see the oncoming headlights.

The rumbling engine is the giveaway. I press myself to a tree and peer through the darkness.

The truck pauses alongside mine.

A door opens and slams, then another.

"What the fuck is this?" a man gripes. "Was this here the other day?"

"I wasn't on patrol out here," another answers. "It's been a week since I've been this way."

"Aw, you were doing so good at getting out of the doghouse."

The second man scoffs.

"Admit it, you're an asshole. You say things at inopportune times."

"Was I supposed to *not* tell the boss that his fly was down?"

"This truck is abandoned. They even left the windows down."

"Fuck that, how many spiders do you think are in there?"

"Are you kidding me?"

"It's a phobia. I can't control it."

A door creaks open. "I think this blanket has mold on it. Anything in the bed?"

"Fucking cobweb-covered boxes. Wait. Oh, fun, soggy bedding."

"Ew. Look in another."

There's a sharp burst of static, then garbled voices on

a radio. It's too faint for me to pick up, and I have to resist the urge to creep closer. I know what it's probably about.

"*Now* we can go have some fun. Let's go."

They make a hasty exit. I exhale and wipe the back of my hand on my forehead. I was sweating. But now, as the truck peels out making a quick U-turn, I allow myself to smile.

They fell for it.

I scramble back down, pausing in the tree line until the truck takes a sharp left into West Falls, then go straight for the truck bed. I climb into it and ignore all the boxes along the left side. People are inherently lazy—there was no way they'd go through all of them if the first few they touched were worthless.

The good stuff was in the center four, and I stack them up and carefully clamber down with them in my arms.

Then, I get to work.

39 ARTEMIS

THIS MIGHT BE the most fun I've had in ages.

I'll have to reevaluate my definition of *fun* later—but for now, as I hit the gas and my bike vibrates beneath me, I can't help but smile.

No one will know.

It's been for-fucking-*ever* since I've been on a bike, and it was fate that the repair shop was just two blocks down from Bow & Arrow. When Reese left to retrieve his truck, I took Saint and Kade down to the mechanic's. It was all boarded up, metal grates pulled down over all the doors, but... well, he probably forgot he used to leave a spare key in a fake rock at the back of the building for me.

Because I used to regularly have issues with my bike. Or my brother's. And the one thing Apollo was *very* firm on? If I broke it, I was not going to use Hell Hound resources to fix it.

That's how I found Jim.

I suspect Jim is long gone, but the key worked for the

back door, and there was my bike. It was almost like Jim knew I'd be back for it at some point, because he left a freaking ribbon bow on the seat.

There were two more tucked away, but they seemed to be in working order, so we took those, too. Best-case scenario, they're Jace's and Wolfe's bikes, and Jim just didn't tag them.

Worst-case scenario, I will have to explain to some random Sterling Falls citizens that their bikes were used to liberate the city. And, uh, pay for further repairs if the bikes survive that long.

Anyway, it's probably fine. The bikes started up easily. Kade tossed a sweatshirt at me before we left, and I put that on over the Kevlar. He and Reese did the same, upping our *inconspicuous* vibes. I don't know if the Cyclopes would give chase if they saw we were dressed for battle.

The excess fabric billows around me, the wind snatching at it with a fierceness that rivals our speed. I push the bike harder and will it to howl through the streets.

Saint and Kade peel away in opposite directions. We'll stoke the fire as hot as we can—until we can't anymore.

It doesn't take long before I find a roadblock. It's manned by armed men. There are concrete barriers in the road, creating a funnel for just one car at a time to go through—and only when they move their truck out of the way. Ah, well. Narrow enough for me.

I lean forward and gun it.

They shout and wave their guns, attempting to stop me.

I swing the rifle, slung by a strap across my back, to my front. One-handed, I brace the butt on my shoulder and flick off the safety. The spray of gunfire takes them by surprise, and I pepper the side of the truck in a flurry of bullets.

They take cover, and I rip through the roadblock, swerving to navigate the tight turns around the concrete barrier and the truck's bumper. One Cyclops is too close to the edge—and too close to grabbing me. I kick out and catch him in the jaw, sending him reeling back into another.

And then I'm around the truck and speeding away, laughing all the while.

Too much fun.

They get their shit together and chase after me, but they're disorganized. They might like exerting power over normal citizens, but they haven't met their match. Bullies never like a fair fight.

I take a sharp turn, then another, continuing west. I come across another roadblock, but it seems like they're better prepared. Maybe they *do* communicate with each other. They're already behind the barriers, their guns aimed. They open fire as soon as they spot my bike. I swerve, sparks jumping up on the asphalt in front of me as their bullets make contact, and hop the curb onto the sidewalk.

There's a cut-through up ahead, maybe thirty yards from the roadblock. It'll dump me out at the next street over, which sounds like a *great* idea. Until I get there and see that it, too, has been blocked completely.

Freaking hell.

The gunfire starts up again, and I press my chest to my bike. It's meant for speed, but the engine whines when I shift gears. I fire back and hit at least two. The rest duck for cover.

They didn't block the sidewalk completely, and I hold my breath as I aim for the gap.

My handlebar on the left goes over the barrier. The right one scrapes the brick wall. Both sides catch at my pants, the outsides of my knees.

Holy shit.

Almost didn't make that.

But I do, and I get the fuck out of there.

They keep shooting. Pain spikes across my back. It forces the air from my lungs. I wheeze, the stab of fear at not being able to breathe almost enough for me to slow. But then, I'm able to inhale.

My bike wobbles, but I hold it steady.

Two blocks left.

A streetlight—red for me—glows up ahead. There are trees just beyond it, the forest beyond West Falls hiding a lot of secrets of its own. But it's also a sign that I'm nearly there.

I approach the last intersection before the light, and I glance over my shoulder. The ones at the roadblock are in the truck, Cyclopes piled in the back and in the cab. The headlights bounce, and it struggles to get up to speed.

I face forward just as another truck—*from the first roadblock*—comes screaming out of the night on my left.

This is déjà vu, and I don't like it.

I hit the brakes, and lean back. My momentum lifts my back tire off the ground. The smell of burning rubber fills my nose, and the truck barely misses me. Like, inches. It skids past, but hell if I stick around.

As soon as my back tire hits the asphalt, I'm off again.

There are shouts behind me, the one truck reversing to give chase, the other one blowing their horn to get them to move. It's a bit of chaos, but that was our goal, right?

With any luck, Kade and Saint are in a similar position. Minus getting shot.

I think I got shot anyway. The adrenaline has blocked out any more pain, and I'm not excited to feel it later.

Ahead, on the road I need to be on, Kade flies by. His head turns, and he automatically slows. I pick up speed and lean into the turn, catching up to him easily.

We didn't put in the comms or anything. Didn't warn Jace, Apollo, or Wolfe about our plan. So I take his *okay* gesture to mean he's all right, and I nod back. We get to the next street, and suddenly Saint shoots out with three vehicles behind him.

Damn, fine.

We catch up, the three of us in a row, and I check back to see who's following.

Two from me. Three from Saint. And Kade managed to goad two more into the chase, too.

We just have to survive the next mile.

"Incoming!" Kade roars.

He leans away, his bike crossing the double yellow line. Gunfire opens up behind us. Saint goes in the opposite direction, and I fucking hesitate.

Another burst of pain, but I can't tell where it came from. My skin is on fire. I groan and cough, and my grip on the handlebars loosens.

No. I shake my head and suck in a breath. No time for passing out or quitting or whatever. We've come so far for that to *not* be the ending.

And then we're passing Reese's truck—the designated line of safety. I brake and swing around, Kade and Saint doing the same. Albeit, a bit more civilized. Reese steps out from behind the truck with a long-barreled rocket launcher on his shoulder. He spares me a glance, checks for Saint and Kade, then focuses on the seven approaching vehicles. They're spread across the road, three-wide. One in front.

He fires, and the whistle of the rocket launcher is alarmingly loud. It catches the grill of the front vehicle.

It explodes. The back end lifts, the whole thing engulfed in flames, and lands on its roof. A second later, the wall of heat pushes into me. It fades, and I flick my visor up.

"Holy shit."

"This isn't over," Reese warns. "But it's about to be."

The other trucks seems to be frozen. If they get away, this is all in vain.

Reese fires again, striking one of the outer vehicles. It jumps off the ground with the force, the ball of fire taking out everyone. It's then that the others suddenly unstick, their engines revving when they're put into reverse. They fly backward.

"They're getting away!"

Reese sets down the rocket launcher and takes his phone from his pocket. He unlocks it and taps the screen, then looks at me.

"No, they're not," he says softly.

One by one, bombs along the road go off. It's a domino effect, and there's no escaping it. No outrunning it. After the second, I cover my ears. Reese pulls me behind the truck, where Kade and Saint await. I count the vibrations.

Ten.

After a long moment, Reese tugs my hands away from my ears. He goes out and checks the damage. Kade immediately follows.

I share a look with Saint.

This wasn't part of the plan. The rocket launcher, yes.

"All clear," Kade says. "Now we see if anyone comes to investigate."

"And if they do?" Saint asks.

Kade peers into the bed of the truck and withdraws a different rifle. This one is more like the kind a sniper would use. "Then we pick them off."

Great.

"One quick question." I clear my throat. "Where did those bombs come from?"

Reese grins. "Um, Gabriel told me where he hid his extras."

"And where was that?" I shake my head. "Scratch that—you trusted him enough to *fetch* them and not get blown up in the process?"

"Well, yeah." Reese shrugs. "They were at Olympus. Guess at one point, his plan was to bring down the building. So in theory, I did you a favor by removing them safely."

"Right..."

Saint throws his arm around my shoulders. "And she means to say thank you, but also you should've brought one of us in case we needed to save *your* ass from a burning building."

I nod vigorously. "Yeah. That."

He laughs. "Okay. Fine. I deserve that."

"Let's clear off the road," Kade says. "Get in the truck in case we need to leave in a hurry."

I exchange a glance with Reese and Saint. The last time we were all pressed together in his truck... Well, it led to some understandings between us.

Reese gets in the driver's seat, and Saint circles to the passenger side.

I look at Kade. "What about you?"

He gestures to the bed. "Gonna set this up on the roof of the cab. Don't worry about me."

Well... that's silly. I suck my lower lip between my teeth, and I don't move. Not until Kade stops what he's doing and hops down from the bed of the truck. He lands right in front of me.

He reaches out and runs his finger along my trapped lower lip. I release it slowly, and he exhales.

"I will worry about you," I say to him. "Okay?"

His dark gaze burns, and he visibly swallows. "Okay."

"ALL THINGS CONSIDERED, I think Lyssa should come back."

I'm met with blank stares. It might be the time—we woke everyone up to have this conversation after we finished with the Cyclopes in West Falls. All I want is to fall into bed. Literally, any bed. But the sun is rising, and I don't see that happening for a while yet.

"What?" I spread my arms. "We have a plan to take out Ouranos. We have dealt with a good chunk of the Cyclopes, and you guys said you'd take over weeding out the rest."

Jace nods slowly, but he still doesn't seem convinced.

I face Kade. "What will Ouranos do if he gets in contact with Gabriel?"

"Use what happened on Isle of Paradise against us," he says.

"*Exactly*. We talked about this. We planned for this. We knew that Ouranos had spies at the trauma center. Gabriel doesn't visit, but he does check up on her a few times a year. All that to say, he doesn't know what happened, and that is *exactly* the thing Ouranos will exploit." I rub my hands together. "Come on, guys. You know I'm right."

Kora clears her throat. Her guys all look at her, but none seem surprised that she has something to say. She holds Wolfe's hand on her thigh, and she meets my gaze.

"You are right," she says. "If he gets in Gabriel's head, the only way to prove *our* side isn't a lie or a manipulation is to show him the truth. The only truth: she's alive and awake."

I narrow my eyes. "I'm sensing a *but*."

"But..." Her cheeks pinken. "I love Sterling Falls, and it's still dangerous. With where she is in her therapy, is it *wise* to remove her from that environment?"

"We can get her anyone she needs," Kade says. "Physical therapy. Speech. Occupational. The trauma center isn't the be-all and end-all."

"It might be setting her back being there," I add quietly. "She was there up until she was torn away and sold to Terror. Since then, Terror is the last place she knew."

"So is it a benefit to keep her somewhere familiar and safe, or a hindrance?" Reese seems more worried than anything. "I don't know."

I bite my cheek and try to stem my frustration. We're at my brother's house, seated around the dining room table once again. At least this time, Kade isn't in zip ties. There are coffee mugs all around. Daniel is missing—he left for Bow & Arrow with Saint to get a jump on rewiring our security system.

The Cyclopes had cut a lot of wires, plus the sheriff's office removed some hardware in their raid... Daniel offered an upgrade, complete with new cameras, internet, and alarms on the doors and windows.

Since Saint volunteered to go with him, his absence is loud, as well.

"Artemis," Vittoria says softly. "I don't know if Gabriel can change."

"What?"

"He has had a long time to become this version of him." She keeps talking so gently, it's making it worse. "Why do you think Lyssa wants to see him? She knew him in Terror—that's it. They trauma-bonded. And when she didn't wake up, it broke him. Sometimes, things just can't be fixed."

Things, like people. *Things*, like Gabriel's mental state.

I was in Terror, too. I was just as lost and afraid as he was.

What if I fell in love in Terror?

My attention shifts to Reese, and my heart skips a beat.

What if Reese fell asleep and never woke up? What if it was Antonio's fault? Would I have blamed him? Would I have—

Reese grabs my hand and squeezes tightly, like he can hear exactly what I'm thinking.

"I believe in him," Reese says to Vittoria. "He's done horrible things, I truly understand that."

He's a victim of Gabriel.

So is Antonio.

Kade.

Saint.

Me.

I absently rub the crook of my elbow. The desire for heroin is always there, but I've been getting better at tuning it out. Right now, it's a screaming need. I want to take it and get the hell out of my own head. I don't want to be in charge, I don't want to *think.*

"Everyone is worth saving," Apollo murmurs. "No one's soul is that far gone. Not when they were so kind in the face of everything that happened to them."

"I remember Gabriel when he came out of Terror," Wolfe says. "He never left Lyssa's side, but he was..."

Kora's expression turns sad.

"He wasn't crazy," Wolfe continues. "He wasn't full of hate or anger. After *years.* That has to count for something, doesn't it?"

"The boy in Terror was gentle." Antonio takes his wife's hand and rubs her knuckles. "He didn't deserve his fate—none of it."

"Putting Lyssa's life in danger should not be up for debate." Vittoria's voice is firm. "I stood by as you brought that *monster* into this house, Artemis. Please don't make me do it again."

A lump forms in my throat. I've never seen kind, sweet Vittoria this upset. She sits tall in her chair, her mouth set in a firm line. She watched her husband come back from agony. He barely survived Gabriel. And, on some level, I understand her stance.

I just don't agree with it.

"It'll be Lyssa's choice," Reese says. "Tem and I will go, we'll just ask her if she wants to see him again. She says no, we come back without her."

I nod quickly.

My brother grimaces. "Okay. When?"

Reese and I exchange a look.

"I need a few hours of sleep," I admit. "We've been up all night."

Jace chokes on his coffee.

"*Not like that!*" I shriek. I cover my face. "Get that image out of your mind, Jace King. We were killing Cyclopes."

Kade snickers, but that's the only sound in the room. I drop my hands and am met with stares.

"Please elaborate," Kora says.

I take a deep breath. "Okay, *well...*"

41 KADE

WE DON'T GET BACK to the club until mid-morning, after the inquisition from Tem's brother and his friends finishes to their satisfaction. Daniel is hard at work, but as soon as we show up with Jace and Wolfe in tow, Saint, Reese, Tem and I make ourselves scarce.

I was expecting a certain level of awkwardness, but both Saint and Reese make faces when I offer to take the couch. Even Artemis rolls her eyes and huffs at me.

She peels my sweatshirt off her body. She's facing me, and that's the only reason I catch her grimace of pain.

"What was that?" I demand.

"Oh." She puts her hand to her back. "Um, I forgot."

Forgot *what?*

She rotates slowly, and my eyes bug out.

There's a bullet in the Kevlar. Upper back and a little off-center. I immediately slide my hand under it, feeling for blood.

Nothing. Still—

"One more," she says. "Lower?"

"Fucking hell, woman." I grit my teeth and bend. The bottom plate in the vest just barely caught it. Another half-inch down and it would've been buried in her spine.

I undo the Velcro straps and help lift it off, then her shirt. Her back is a patchwork of deep-purple bruises.

Saint and Reese come over, and both of them make noises of disapproval.

"You got shot and you're just telling us about it now?" Saint demands.

Tem rolls her eyes. "The vest caught it. You're saying you didn't even catch a stray bullet? Loser."

Saint scowls.

Reese grabs the sweatshirt she was wearing and finds the two holes, sticking his fingers through them. "Your brother is going to kill you."

She laughs, then winces. "Yeah. Ow. I was fine up until right now."

"Shocker," I mutter. "Adrenaline does that."

"We were sitting at my brother's..."

"And you were up in arms defending Gabriel," I finish. "Do you keep painkillers around? Medicine cabinet?"

Tem stiffens. "Am I allowed to take that?"

"Tylenol?" Saint questions. "I think that's allowed, Artemis."

Ooh, he full-named her. With his memory back, I think he saves *Artemis* for emergencies. Like when she gets shot and doesn't tell us.

"Tylenol and waters all around," Reese says. "And then we're going to sleep."

"Thank goodness." Tem undoes her pants and drops them.

My eyebrows hike, but she doesn't bat an eye. She fills four glasses with water, dropping a few cubes of ice into each, and passes them around. Saint comes back with a small bottle of ibuprofen, and he taps out some for all of us.

"Cheers," Tem mutters.

We clink glasses and take our pain relievers.

I follow them into the bedroom, pausing when Reese goes to one side and Saint the other. Tem climbs straight down the middle, drawing her legs up to tuck them under the sheet and blankets.

"Come on," Saint says gruffly. "You can be the big spoon."

He leaves room for me on the edge, scooting close to Artemis. She's framed in by Reese and Saint, sharing a pillow with the former. I drop my pants, too—the last to do so—and flick the light off. I take my time closing the blinds, then slowly crawl in behind Saint.

I wish I could say I savor it, but the military taught me to sleep wherever and whenever I could. As a result, I'm out in seconds.

I WALK OUT OF BOW & Arrow and examine the barren street.

Artemis and Reese left on their errand a little while ago, and the rest of us have busied ourselves cleaning up the place.

The bodies are gruesome in the light of day. Cyclopes just following orders.

They were given the chance to surrender, I remind myself.

I guess part of me expected Ouranos to send someone to collect them, but so far... nothing. And since there's no unusual activity on the street, I duck back inside and lock the door behind me.

My body is sore from holding extra tension. The sun is setting. My stomach growls, but I ignore it. Movement will be the best cure for my physical wellbeing, and the last I heard, Jace, Wolfe, and Saint were playing cards in one of the private rooms. Daniel was hanging around them, too, finishing the security shit.

They didn't seem inclined to include me, but I have been perfectly content on my own. No need to force a square peg into a round hole.

Unless the square peg is my cock, and the round hole is Saint's asshole, of course. Then, with the right amount of lube, anything is possible.

Even though I fell asleep fast, I dreamt of Saint and Artemis. And when I woke up just after two o'clock in the afternoon, I was alone with a raging boner. There was a plate of food left on the table for me, with instructions in Tem's handwriting for how long to microwave it.

After I ate every last bite, I went to work. I didn't

want to bother Saint, Jace, and Wolfe, and I guess waking up solo was a sign for me to continue the day that way.

I go to the back stairwell, the one that leads from the ground floor up to the top-floor offices—and Tem's apartment, somewhere in between the two, which we're now more intimately familiar with after our nap—and roll my shoulders back.

I jog up to the top, drop and do fifteen push-ups, then jog down. Crunches at the bottom. I repeat the cycle, getting faster on the stairs, swinging around the landings to keep momentum. On my fourth lap, a sheen of sweat covers my face, neck, shoulders, and back.

On the fifth, my legs tremble with every down step.

Sixth, and I become aware of an audience.

Saint.

"Lurking? Or do you want to join me?"

He steps out of the shadows and smirks. "You could join *me*... I was headed to the shower."

I raise my eyebrow. Last night was about Artemis, which I appreciate. I'll never get sick of that woman's body, even hidden under too much fabric. Or seeing her with Saint, for that matter. But we haven't really discussed his memory, which is clearly back.

I apologized to Reese, but Saint and Tem need to hear it, too. Although I have a feeling Saint will forgive me quick, and Artemis will make me beg for it.

That's okay. I'd get on my knees for her any time.

He seems to know that I'm off my game, because my lack of an answer has him smiling wider. "Come on."

I wet my lips. "What about Artemis?"

"She's supportive of our... endeavors." He winks. "She just wants a play-by-play later."

Oh, fuck.

"Daniel, Jace, and Wolfe left, so it's just us," he adds.

He strides by me and climbs the stairs. I stare after him for another moment, then come to my damn senses. I take the steps two at a time to catch up with him—or rather, linger a few steps below to admire his ass—and follow him into Tem's apartment.

It's empty. He yanks his shirt off and tosses it over his shoulder. It hits me in the chest, and I automatically catch it. My gaze is drawn to his naked, muscled back. Tattoos cover it, disappearing into the waistband of his jeans. The placements are impeccable, each one moving with the lines of his body.

I drop his shirt and lose mine, too. I kick off my shoes, tug off socks, and unbutton my pants, my dick already hardening in anticipation.

He's just in jeans, too, by the time we reach the bathroom. He goes in and starts the water, and he's barely turned around when I pounce.

I kiss him hard, pressing my body to his. My skin wakes up at the contact, my dick straining against my jeans. He shifts, widening his stance, and grasps at my waist. He kisses back just as fierce, his teeth snagging my lower lip and biting down. I groan at the bloom of pain and the way the sensation goes straight to my groin.

He's hard, too. His hips move, shifting against me, and I feel it pressing on my thigh.

His hand sweeps up from my waist, over my nipple, and comes to a rest over my heart. Where his tattoo is.

He drags his lips from mine and looks down at it, blinking. "You didn't tell me about this. When my mind was all fucked up."

"No," I agree.

He meets my gaze. "Why?"

Why, indeed?

"Because I didn't want that to influence you." I catch his chin in my hand so he can't turn away. "I didn't realize, when you first came into Hawthorne's office, that you had forgotten. But I had been looking for you..."

Because Ouranos wanted you dead.

Still does, probably. I would say I've effectively cut ties with the man after last night. There's no going back.

"I caught a glimpse of you walking down the hall and thought I was seeing things," I confess.

Saint leans in until our lips are almost touching. He keeps his eyes on mine, and I revel in his newfound confidence. Like restoring the two years' worth of memories has given him back his shine.

I can recall the way he blushed on the beach beside that house in North Falls, his gaze dropping to my cock and then quickly away. Or the way he fought—let's not forget that. We were strangers back then, but he moved with savage beauty.

"Well, thanks for not manipulating me too much," he says.

I huff a laugh, then quickly fall silent when he grabs

my dick through my jeans. He squeezes and tugs lightly, smirking at me. My reaction.

"These should come off," he says.

He finishes dragging my zipper down and pulling both the denim and briefs down my hips, thighs. He crouches, guiding my feet out, then looks up at me.

"Hmm." He leans in and opens his mouth.

Oh, fuck.

He slides the tip of my cock past his lips, and warm wetness envelops my length. His tongue flicks at my piercings, then dips deeper. I lean forward and brace myself on the wall behind him as he tastes me.

It's clear he's never done this before, but he doesn't seem to have any problem exploring.

Or experimenting.

He sucks, his cheeks hollowing. His hand comes up, and he grasps me. He twists his hand, the pressure tight and a perfect combination. I imagine this is how he likes it. A blending of sensations.

When he lifts my balls in his other hand, I let out a hiss. Everything is so damn sensitive, and I can't ruin it by jacking my hips forward. It's what I want to do—I want to grab on to his hair and shove him down, to take control and show him how I can fuck a face.

His face.

He pulls off and tips his head back, his eyes half-lidded. "Go on, then."

It's like he heard me.

I touch his cheek, briefly. I slide my fingers through his hair to the back of his head and drag him back to my cock. This isn't exactly how I wanted it to go—I wanted to be inside him. But I can't resist this either. I fill his mouth, plunging deeper until I hit the back of his throat. His eyes widen.

"There you go," I breathe. "Relax into it."

He does. His throat works, squeezing at my tip, until I pull back. His nostrils flare with his sharp inhale, and I do it again. I get into a rhythm, making sure he's not hating it. His hand is in his pants, freeing his dick. I grunt when he jacks himself.

Selfishly, I don't want him to come in his hand. I pick up my pace, and he mirrors me. I've got the leg up on him. The advantage of his mouth and a head start in the race.

My balls tighten, and I tell him I'm about to come a split second before my climax hits.

He swallows, nearly choking on it. His tongue sweeps around my length as I pull out.

"Hands off," I grit out.

He releases himself. His rock-hard cock bobs in the air, tattooed and perfect. I step back, eyeing him. He wipes his mouth on the back of his hand and narrows his eyes.

I smile, then turn away to fix the water temperature. I climb in without a backward glance, the hot water immediately pummeling my chest. I rotate and tip my head into the stream.

Saint doesn't take long to join me, entering from the opposite end. The curtain rustles back into position when he is fully in, and my gaze drifts across his body. He's ripped. His abdominal muscles flex under my inspection. His cock is still hard, pointing at me.

Poor thing.

And he wasn't taken care of last night either.

The sacrificial Saint.

I step closer, into his space, until our chests bump. He has to look up at me like this, the slightest incline of his chin, and I smirk down at him. I lean in, so fucking slow, and press my lips to his.

He doesn't hesitate to kiss me back, and my fucking heart soars. I reach between us and grip his length. His hips buck once, then still. I jerk him off, my wet hand sliding easily. I know how *I* like it, and I have a feeling he likes a solid grip, too. He pants into my mouth.

"Not yet," I say, my breath mixing with his.

He grunts. He grasps at my waist, and his nails dig in the more I stroke him. When his grip tightens, I release his cock. I plunge my tongue in his mouth and take my time tasting him. He fights back, and I revel in the passion.

He has come back. The memory-lacking Saint wouldn't be this into it. Not with months of sexual tension from the *old* him under his belt.

No belt on anymore…

With that in mind, I break our kiss and drop to my knees. He tasted me, now I want to show him what *I* can do. He opens and closes his mouth, but I just wink at him. The water hits the back of my neck and runs down my back.

"Oh, fuck," Saint murmurs.

"Let me show you how to suck a dick like it's your favorite flavor," I say.

I grab his hand and put it on the back of my head, then I open my mouth and swallow him whole.

"IS THAT TEM?"

Saint's voice is raspy. His fingers trace a pattern across my back, randomly pressing into the muscles when he finds a knot. It's been a luxury, in a way, to be able to just exist with him for the last few hours. The shower blow job led to washing each other, and more kissing, but that's it. We fell into bed, but it was exhaustion-driven, not sexual.

He's referring to the chime from my phone, which I haven't yet looked at. My phone is on the floor, and one of my arms hangs off it. My fingers are inches from the device.

But checking seems like bursting this quiet bubble, and I hesitate.

It chimes again, which is probably not very Tem-like, at all. I'm not actually sure Artemis knows where her phone is.

I groan and flip my phone screen-up, tapping to wake it up.

Ouranos.

My eyes open, my body waking up. "Fuck."

I shove myself up and swing my legs over the edge of the bed. Saint's hand falls away, but I ignore him to hunt for my underwear and jeans. I slide them on, then my shoes, and fumble for a shirt.

Pretty sure it's Saint's shirt, but whatever.

"It's not Tem," I say. "I'll be back."

Phone in hand, I hastily exit her apartment and jog upstairs. I pass her office, then Antonio's, and am in the kitchen when my phone starts trilling with an incoming call.

I slip out into the open rooftop bar and answer it.

"Your message was received loud and clear," Ouranos says without preamble. His voice is deep, but he doesn't sound annoyed, exactly. "My Cyclopes were discovered outside of Bow & Arrow, which I assume you've taken over."

I cock my head. Why isn't he mentioning the seven cars' worth of men we killed last night? We did a great job cleaning up the mess, but you'd think he would've noticed that many gone.

Well, actually, his Cyclopes never checked in with him. It was always me or Gabriel who they reported to... Would he have been able to reach everyone?

Perhaps this is just a delay. A delightful delay in him receiving information.

"Kade." His voice shifts into something darker. "Are you going to deny it?"

I straighten. "No, I don't deny it. We've taken over the club... and everything below it."

He lets out a laugh. "You think you can hold that space? My men are all across the city. I might not want it today, Kade, but I *will* be coming for Terror."

He really doesn't know.

A thrill goes through me, but I'm not about to be the one to reveal it. I'll let that honor go to someone more deserving. Artemis, perhaps. They haven't ever come face-to-face, but I think she might relish telling him a chunk of his army was wiped out with one hastily built plan.

"Does this have to do with Artemis or Reese?" He pauses. "Or is it Saint Hart? I saw your expression when I mentioned him before."

Is there a nice way of saying *all three?*

He sighs. "Oh, Kade. You've always had an issue leading from your heart instead of your brain."

"I—"

"Here's the deal," he continues as if I hadn't tried to speak. "I don't really give a shit about you. Your leadership skills were good in Emerald Cove, but I'm looking for a bit more. Who I *do* want is Gabriel. So, you tell me where he is, and I won't send every single fucking person under my command to North Falls and burn the whole club to the ground."

There it is: the reason for the call. He knows I'm not on his side, but he still thinks he can get another ounce of information from me.

Gabriel and I are connected through Lyssa. That's been the one thread keeping us connected. She's awake, and the guy who calls me his brother has no fucking idea. She's hidden under a different name, relearning how to live again. To use her muscles. To walk. To eat solid food.

She'll be okay. My dear sister is going to live.

Will Gabriel?

I thought I could trust him, but he attacked Saint...

"He's no longer with us," I say evenly. "But I'm pretty sure I know where he is."

I give Ouranos an address and hang up before I can regret it.

Across the restaurant, mostly concealed by shadows, someone pushes off the wall. They give me a slow wave before they leave. The door swings shut behind them, and I turn away.

"Good luck," I whisper.

42 GABRIEL

"LET *GO!*"

They listen, and I'm tossed rather unceremoniously onto the floor. I take my time picking myself up, my heart hammering.

"There you are, Gabriel," Ouranos says.

He always says that with a tone of surprise, like he didn't expect me to turn up. I didn't *turn up*—I was cornered by his goons in South Falls and dragged here. I run my fingers through my hair, pushing it out of my face, and straighten my clothes. White graphic t-shirt that says *Anarchy*. Jeans. Boots. I had a sweatshirt and jacket, but they got lost somewhere along the way. In the struggle.

My body aches, but the bright prick of pain comes from my cheekbone. Not the side that he ground into the glass, of course. No, now I'll have matching mismatched wounds. The cuts have scabbed over. This isn't a gash, its just swollen.

One of them broke the bone, I think.

Stupid sheep. They'll pay for that one. Over and over. Their faces are imprinted in my mind. Even if I'm not the favorite—

"You helped Artemis take her club back," he says idly.

Oh, right. I suppose that puts me on the outs with Ouranos, doesn't it? That's why I didn't go crawling back to him after giving Saint a little bop. I went and tried to get onto Isle of Paradise, only for Bobby to basically drive away without me. He took one look at me coming down the dock and unhooked his mammoth houseboat as fast as possible, which was kind of impressive. He was out of reach by the time I got to his section.

Dick-face.

All I know is that there's something wrong on Isle of Paradise, the trauma center has been compromised, and Lyssa... I don't *know*. I felt something was wrong, didn't I? I felt it when I was holding the Hell Hounds leader guy's body under the water and watching him try to gurgle with a punctured lung. It was like—

What if she's dead?

What if that feeling was her saying goodbye?

"Are you with me, Gabriel?"

Back to Ouranos. If she *is* dead, he'd be a good one to go to in order to also get dead. He kind of has a murderous rage about him, but it only appears at random. Like when he has to deal with me and I can't quite focus on his words.

I blink at him.

I betrayed him, didn't I? That usually means death. A

quick shot to the back of the head—or the front, depending on how pissed he is. Except, he's not usually the one pulling the trigger. He has guys for that. Cyclopes. And they all went *boom.*

He's blissfully unaware of that, too. Even the guys who snatched me were quiet. Confident. There's got to be more Cyclopes in the city, but who really knows? Kade was in charge of personnel. I doubt he was keeping a literal ledger, though.

The important thing is that they took out a few. Like, thirty. Maybe forty.

That's a lot of death swinging over the head of sweet Artemis. Kind of like a guillotine of guilt, in a way. Or a pendulum. Guillotines don't swing.

A sharp pendulum on a fraying rope, sweeping closer and closer to her delicate neck.

Poor bird.

Speaking of—

"I want to see Lyssa," I say.

He scoffs. "You won't be seeing her any time soon. Of that, I'm sure."

"Why?"

"Because as soon as you double-crossed me, I had her moved."

My eye twitches. "Where?"

He laughs. He's dressed impeccably, like always. Like the city hasn't begun to burn around him in ways he cannot control. He reminds me of the men who used to frequent Terror. I'm surprised it took me this long...

No, wait.

The men who came to Terror, who paid for me, were in charge. I learned that early on, and no form of therapy —*trust me, I tried it*—would shake that. So when I came upon Ouranos, it was natural that I bent my neck for him.

But the one thing that always straightened my spine? *Lyssa.*

I simply forgot, with her being asleep. But now he's denying me again—*you cannot go*—and my spine is straightening. It's about time I grew a fucking backbone.

"You knew I betrayed you, so you moved her," I echo him. "And you won't tell me where she is. The love of my life. The one thread keeping me from insanity. You think the best idea is to hide her from me?"

"I will give her to you once you help me," Ouranos amends. "Kill Kade. Extinguish the hope that Artemis Madden and her family have ignited around this city, and you can go be with Lyssa."

You're a rabid dog on a chain. Kade once said that to me. In passing. When we first got to Sterling Falls and the rest of my mask chipped and fell off. Or maybe he mumbled it when I put the needle through the man's eye. Or as I hung another from the outside of Bow & Arrow. Or when he found my room full of bomb-making material.

Alas, I focused too much on the rabid part. The frenzy, the chaos, the inability to control myself when I really got going.

I failed to acknowledge the chain.

And who held the other end of it.

"Do you think you control me?" I cock my head. I

brush my hands down my shirt. "Truly? Order me to bark—"

"And you'll bark," Ouranos finishes without hesitation.

He *does* think he controls me.

A laugh trickles out of me, the lightness in my chest akin to slurping a cold fizzy drink. Bubbles everywhere. Up my nose, in my throat. It's *delightfully* painful. The kind of discomfort that comes with joy.

Until right this moment, he was probably right. He did control me. But there was someone else, too. Someone with a deeper hold driving my motivation.

And right now, Ouranos is trying to use her against me.

"What does Artemis have to do with your plans?" My curiosity has gotten the better of me.

He tenses, and that gives him away.

He lunges forward, his arm swinging. I watch it coming, but I don't move. His palm collides with my cheek at a startlingly fast rate, and my head whips to the side. The explosion of pain is more severe than I expected, and my vision flickers. I lose touch with my body for a split second. When it comes back, I'm on the floor. On my hands and knees.

I forgot about my broken cheekbone.

He hauls me up by the back of my shirt. He catches sight of the gun holster hidden in the small of my back— *empty*—and he tuts. He shoves me away and slowly undoes his cufflinks. I watch him, blinking fast, while he rolls up his sleeves.

"This is all to teach me a lesson, isn't it?" I laugh, bleeding effervescence. "I forgot about lessons."

"You'll remember," he promises.

I straighten just as he comes at me again. He punches me in the gut. My stomach heaves, my breath comes out in a *whoosh* of forced air. Everything in me seizes up when I can't immediately draw in another breath.

Relax. I fight against the panic. This is natural. I've been here before. I used to relish it, and I catch the feeling with both hands. Metaphorically speaking.

I let the absence of air sharpen me. His elbow comes down on my back, knocking me back to my knees.

A familiar place.

I rock back on my heels and look up at him, choking on air. I draw in a ragged inhale, then another. "You want me to suck your cock? You didn't have to go through so much trouble—"

He strikes again, this time his fist on my mouth. Blood spills across my tongue. I spit it out and cackle. The metallic taste is sharp. It's all I can smell.

Idiot.

For once, he is disheveled. There's blood on his knuckles—*mine*—and his hair has fallen out of its gelled obedience. His chest heaves, the effort of teaching me this very important *lesson* weighing on him. The physical exertion of inflicting pain should not be taken for granted.

I laugh and shove myself to my feet, hollow chest and bones be damned.

I stagger, and he allows it. He lets me put my hand on the bar, slide my palm along the smooth wood, and catch a pint glass. It has the barest amount of liquid in the bottom, and I overturn it. The pale-yellow ale splatters across the floor.

"You forget yourself, old man." I smile, then widen it. Wider. Lips and cheeks stretching, straining, until he can see every tooth. My cheek screams at me. I slam the glass against the edge of the bar, and it fractures. Another hit, and the pieces tumble to the floor to join the beer.

He is not wary—he's mad. "Do not destroy my things, Gabriel. We've talked about this. Your lashing out has come to an end."

"Perhaps."

He comes at me again, and I don't stop him. I want to be at the brink of death. To see my shallow grave. Just because.

He hits and kicks, striking until I'm hunched on the floor, curled in to protect myself. My fingers grasp on the concrete, sorting through the mess, shifting the pieces of glass that bite my skin.

He comes around to my front, his polished black loafers gleaming. He lifts his foot and kicks at my stomach.

I grab his ankle. My body jerks. He tries to free himself, but I've always prided myself on my grip. One hand to secure it, my fingers digging into his skin just above his loafer, the other hand with the broken shard of glass. Before he can dislodge me, I cut the back of his ankle as deeply as I can. Through muscle and tendon.

Release.

Roll.

He howls, but I'm out of his blast radius.

Speaking of that...

I force myself to my feet and round the bar. Behind me, Ouranos crashes into the stools. He yells, his anger directed at me, but I ignore it. He stays even with me, dragging his leg. He can't put weight on it anymore. Perhaps he could, actually, but it would hurt.

"Does that hurt more than finding out your brother was killed by being shot in the face?"

He spits curses and threats, but there's the width of the bar between us.

He's easy to block out. I pause at the bucket of ice, then take two quick steps to the left. I duck down and retrieve the flip phone I had dropped the last time I was here. It was gently toed under the bar, out of sight...

When I stand, Ouranos is swinging for me again.

I bob out of the way and tsk at him, and his expression flashes. Fury. He thought he had me. He's *had* me this whole time, and now I avoid?

I move farther down, catching the glint of a utensil, and nearly crow at the huge fucking knife waiting for me. It whispers a sweet hello when it meets my palm. The next time Ouranos comes at me, I take his hand.

He screams.

And, truth be told, I need a few whacks to get the blade all the way through. It's a big knife, but it's not a miracle worker. Who knows the last time this thing was sharpened? I grip his fingers, trapping his arm on the bar, and I chop. Finally, it comes free and he falls backward. He lands on his ass in the middle of Madness.

Funny, that's right where I've been all along.

He sputters, but he seems to be losing steam. Maybe it's the blood pouring out of his wrist. He'll bleed out in minutes if he doesn't contain it, but I'm not a paramedic. What am I supposed to do, give him orders?

There was my blood and glass, but now there's a lot of his blood. It's all over. It soaks his shirt and pants, pools on the hardwood under him. He finally presses the stump against his stomach, but he's really pale.

There's also the ankle injury.

I wrinkle my nose. "Your lesson is messy."

I come around the bar with his hand in my grasp.

"Lyssa is a curious threat," I tell him. "You know I carry her with me? That I have for a decade?"

He keeps trying desperately to stop the bleeding, but every shift of his weight, every squirm, dislodges his arm and opens it right up again.

You cannot go, he said to me.

I listened.

It doesn't matter. His end is coming.

His end is now.

I crouch in front of him and show him his hand. When he doesn't stop with the noises, I grab a rag and come back. He moves to take it, but I shake my head sharply. I shove the rag into his mouth, and *finally*, there's a little quiet.

Back to the hand. I focus on his manicured nails. He doesn't even have calluses. How out of touch is that?

I fold his fingers down until only the middle one remains, although it's not really staying. It takes me a minute of finagling to get it into the right shape, but I can't let go.

"You're flipping yourself off," I tell him. "That's fun, isn't it?"

When he doesn't react—well, he doesn't laugh, but he keeps moaning—I slap him with the hand. It makes a wet clap when it connects. He doesn't even spit out the rag.

I tap my chin with his extended finger. "Lyssa was named after a fury. I imagine you probably didn't know that, right? You could've looked into that, but why go any deeper than her name? Lyssa. The goddess of mad rage. I took that and I intertwined it with what they did to her— they made her *sleep*. Not sweet Artemis, of course. Just for the record, I forgive her. It's the people who were running Terror who were responsible. The doctors who examined us, the ones who came up with those foul drugs. The ones who decided heroin would be a good way to placate the unruly."

Lyssa and Hypnos. Fury and Sleep. Of course, we're sort of crossing mythologies here. I have no idea if they interacted, and Lyssa isn't technically the Greek spelling.

Whatever.

"Anywho!" I rise. "This is goodbye, Marcus Graves. I wish we could've played a little longer, but... I've got places to be. And I'm bored, to be honest. You haven't been the epitome of exciting. You haven't even been *slightly* entertaining. The screaming and moaning. The hitting. You followed that playbook to a T. I'll give you that.

"What I won't give you is your hand. That'll be my

evidence. I'd take your head, but there's something about what comes next that just gets me all jazzed. Are you ready?"

He stares at me. His nostrils flare, but he doesn't say anything else. I'm sure he'll spit out the rag as soon as I leave, and he'll call for help, and *blah, blah, blah.*

It's too late.

I leave him on the floor and exit through the front door, the hand still in my grasp. May as well take it, right? I stuff it in my back pocket, the fingers bending unhelpfully. The two Cyclopes who dragged me in are still there, leaning against the front and smoking. They take a look at me, then double take, but I'm already moving away.

They don't really give a shit about me. They'll probably take their time finishing the butt before returning to their boss, and by then it'll be too late. He's losing so much blood...

The street is empty. It's broad fucking daylight and it's *empty.* That's gotta be some sort of sin in Sterling Falls, even if it's winter. We're in the middle of a heat wave, I think.

Or, we're about to be.

I cross to the far sidewalk and slow my steps. I pull out the flip phone and hold down the 1 button, triggering my saved speed dial. Just like the old days.

The *boom* of the bomb, which is tucked in the final box of bombs I made *ages* ago, is probably not quite "like the old days."

The sound hits first.

A split second later, a hot blast rushes through me. The back of my neck burns for a moment, and I imagine —without turning around—that the flames are reaching for me.

But, no. I'm far enough away. Out of the radius. The Cyclopes Ouranos had hanging around the front of the building, though...

Well, they probably got caught in it.

I touch my cheek and huff. They deserve it.

My pace quickens as I approach the end of the block. I round the corner, scanning the road. My feet stop, body freezing, before my brain catches up.

There's a familiar car parked on the curb. The one whose trunk I was *un*ceremoniously tossed in by the ever-sweet Artemis. She's stronger than she looks, that Artemis.

I blink rapidly.

Leaning against the back bumper is a phantom.

Okay, maybe I did get caught in the blast. My body is probably back on the sidewalk, half-burnt, and my spirit just kept walking. To an afterlife I don't deserve.

Her arms are crossed over her chest. She's wearing jeans.

Did I ever see her in jeans?

Her sweatshirt has the Cyclops logo on the breast. *She drew that when she was a kid,* I recall. Kade offered it to Ouranos when they were trying to expand. Said he could use it so guys on the same side could recognize each other without *knowing* each other.

It's unique. As unique as her eyes, which are open.

Of course they're open. She's dead, and so am I.

It's not that I expected a shiny afterlife... I was kind of counting on the opposite. Hell, burning, forever tormented, that sort of thing.

"Gabriel."

Her voice doesn't sound the same. It sounds different. Deeper, raspier. But the way she says it is like out of my memories. When she did finally talk to me anyway. There was a time when she wouldn't. Couldn't.

"Stop staring at me."

I picked the wrong Greek god. It comes to me all of a sudden, this idea that's been living under my skin for years. I was never supposed to be Hypnos.

A freaking lightbulb just went off over my head.

I slink forward and lick my lips. I taste more blood—that's probably the punishment, then. I'll bear the pain of a broken cheekbone and a split lip and some loose teeth forever. But I can't not say anything. She started it by saying my name, so... I should say her name.

"Did you ever learn about Orpheus?" is what comes out.

Her brows pinch together. A silent *no*.

He's me, I almost say.

"His beloved was killed. Brutally ripped from him on their wedding night. So, he ventured to the underworld and begged Hades to let her go with him back to the living." I suck in a breath and take another step. It's like my feet are trapped in mud, it's hard to move toward her. "He told Orpheus to follow the path out of the underworld. He said that Eurydice would walk in his footsteps, in his shadow. Following right behind. But if he called out to her, or if he looked back, it would be all for naught. When his shadow passed into the sunlight, she would be there."

My throat works. I don't want to say this next part, but I have to.

"He was *steps* from the light when he looked back at her."

She shakes her head, her expression sad. "Is that why you didn't visit?"

"If I looked back, you would've died," I say. "And now, I'm sorry to say, I failed. You died, didn't you? And I've just killed myself. That's why you're here, isn't it? You're going to escort me to whatever fate awaits us."

Lyssa pushes off the bumper and steps toward me. Her gait is wobbly, her legs shaking like a newborn dear's. I spring forward and catch her forearms, steadying her. She's solid. I hold tight and loose at the same time, because how tight is *too* tight? How much of my strength will hurt her?

"I'm alive," she says. "And so are you."

How did that lump get in my throat? It won't let me swallow. I try, a few times, but all I end up doing is clicking my tongue.

"I... you..."

Lyssa laughs.

I flinch like she slapped me. It's a new sound. One that she couldn't have done... I don't know this sound. I could not have imagined it. I mean, okay, I *have* imagined it, I've theorized and agonized over what the sound could be. This wasn't it. It wasn't that.

Her laugh is the sort of sound that could give a wretched soul like mine a clean start.

"You're here."

She looks up at me. Same blonde hair, but longer. Same hazel eyes, but a bit less haunted. Or maybe more. I can't tell. I don't know. Is she a stranger?

"I'm here," she confirms.

I drag her into me. She wraps her arms around my waist, and I do the same around her shoulders.

And all at once, I'm crying.

43 ARTEMIS

GABRIEL IS COVERED IN BLOOD. His cheek is an ugly mess, the bruising and swelling growing by the second. He sits at the kitchen table in Kora's house, letting me clean the cut on his lip with antiseptic. Although it must burn, he doesn't move a muscle.

Lyssa sits across from him.

He's focused on her, staring like if he blinks, she's going to evaporate. He didn't look away from her in the car, even as he helped her in and roughly wiped away the tears left on his cheeks. He seems to be in shock.

Imagine if Lyssa didn't agree to come with me?

"Oh." Gabriel frowns. "I have this."

He reaches into his pocket and pulls something out. It isn't until the object makes a dull, *wet* thump on the table that I turn my attention to it.

I choke. "That's a hand."

"Ouranos," he says solemnly. "Proof of death."

My mouth opens and closes.

"Tem." Saint comes into the room. He eyes Gabriel, then nearly chokes at the sight of the hand on the table.

"Oh, good." I motion to it. "You think you can get that... uh, identified?"

He shakes his head. "No. I'm not touching that thing. Whose is it?"

"Ouranos," Gabriel says. "Obviously. Look at the ring."

I focus on the bloody fingers again. The flat, circular ring on the pinky. Freaking pretentious, is what it is. There's an engraving on the surface, but I can't make it out. And, frankly, I have no desire to lean in closer.

"That's not what I came in here for," Saint says.

Lyssa makes a face.

"Spit it out, then," I say on a sigh. "I'm not sure I can handle any more bad news."

He cracks a smile. "It's not bad news."

I straighten. "Really?"

"We found Malik."

Gabriel makes a face. I press a little harder with the gauze on his cheek, and he snatches my wrist.

"*Ow*," he snaps.

"Where is Malik?" I demand.

"Hospital." Saint shakes his head. "He was checked in as John Doe, that's why we haven't been able to find him."

"And?" My breath catches. "Is he okay?"

Malik Barlow has been the last puzzle piece. He wasn't at Bow & Arrow when we raided it, like Gabriel suggested. He wasn't anywhere.

Gabriel sighs. "The minions probably brought him there when Ouranos said to keep him alive."

I scowl and shove my chair back. It's either that or take out my anger on him, and what would that solve? It might make me feel better for a few seconds, but it wouldn't rewind time.

"You never visited me," Lyssa says.

She's been in all sorts of therapies—speech, physical, occupational—and while her speech is still somewhat disjointed, she's made massive improvements. She's improved in all areas, actually.

"I... didn't," he murmurs. "No. I did not."

"I remember all of it."

Uh-oh. "Um, what does that mean?" I interject.

Her gaze flicks to me, and she carefully tucks her light-blonde hair behind her ear. "Locked-in Syndrome. Means you're conscious but... stuck."

My eyes widen.

Saint coughs. "Damn, Lyssa."

Her lips curl. "So that means all the shit Tem told me..."

"Oops." I flash Saint a sheepish smile and sidle towards him. "So, um, where are Kade and Reese?"

"What shit did Tem tell you?"

She lifts a shoulder and mimes zipping her lips.

Thanks, I mouth at her.

"We should let them talk," I tell Saint. I take his hand and tow him toward the door. "Jace can babysit. He owes me."

"He owes you for what?" Saint chases after me.

"For putting up with *you*." I laugh.

He grabs my hips and picks me up mid-stride. I squeak, but he doesn't falter when he tosses me over his shoulder.

He palms my ass, his chuckle vibrating through me. "I'll show you putting up with me."

You know what? I'll happily accept that.

44 REESE
TWO MONTHS LATER

I BLOW out a slow breath and look up at the house. It was a foundation a few weeks ago, and then a skeleton of framing, and now... it's a *house*. The air smells like saltwater, and wide windows in the back of said house give gorgeous views of the ocean. The siding is finished, the blue-gray color striking against the backdrop of ocean and sand. The interior is finished, as of the contractor's army of trucks pulling away a few minutes ago.

Artemis burned down the last house that stood here.

And Saint's first love died somewhere around where I'm standing.

But when Kade proposed building something new on this property for the four of us, his cheeks flushed, Saint didn't object.

And our golden girl has no idea.

But I think she'll be okay with it—she likes to build over her trauma.

Speaking of, she's been busy rebuilding Bow & Arrow and helping Kora get Elodie settled back into Sterling Falls. Saint, Jace, Wolfe, and Apollo have been working on clearing out the rest of the Cyclopes imbedded in the city.

The sheriff's sister is awake—and so is the sheriff. And Malik Barlow, for that matter. Still not sure I like him, especially since he barged into my life and threatened to keep Artemis away from me... but that was months ago.

Pre-invasion.

Kade wipes the sweat from his brow with the hem of his shirt. He has some new artwork across his chest and biceps, curtesy of Saint. The latter has split his time between helping his friends and repairing his tattoo shop. The huge front window was smashed in at some point, and there was graffiti across the walls. Some of his stuff was stolen.

The devastation on his face...

But the people responsible are gone or dead, and that has to be enough while he cleans up the place. He tattooed a vine going up Tem's leg, from her foot up to her hip. It has thorns and flowers alike, and it moves with her so well it seems almost part of her.

Gotta say, I'm really freaking glad the dude got his memory back. There was a darkness in him for a while. I imagine that's the Saint that Artemis had to deal with after Nyx was first killed and Jace asked him to live with her.

At least Kade and I were able to run *some* sort of

interference on that front. Kade was more effective at getting Saint to cut it out, but I was always down to comfort Tem when it got to be too much.

How did she handle it alone the first time around?

"You've got a look on your face," Kade says.

I scowl. "No, I don't."

"The surprise is going to go over like a rainbow."

"That is not a saying." I glare at him. "You've been hanging out with Gabe too much."

Kade just shrugs.

And that's another thing—*Gabriel*. And Lyssa.

Shortly after the whole holy-shit-she's-awake reveal, she opted to return to Isle of Paradise. And, the most surprising plot twist of all: Gabriel opted to go, too.

And that lasted approximately six weeks before he got kicked out.

Guess a psycho can't truly ever change their stripes.

Anyway—Kade got the late-night phone call from Dr. Hawthorne, demanding someone come get Gabe immediately. That she was at her wits' end and was going to chuck him into the ocean if he stayed another night.

Maybe she didn't say it like *that*, but I like to read between the lines.

So Kade and Gabe have been crashing together in Tem's condo, while Tem, Saint, and I have been sleeping at the Bow & Arrow apartment. I'm pretty sure Kade would rather be plastered in bed with us, but he's been deemed Gabe's babysitter.

And yes, I call him Gabe purely to irritate him. Even in my inner monologue.

"We shouldn't order furniture, right?" Kade asks.

"Right..." I head up the newly set stone walkway and go inside. It smells fresh and new and like drying paint. The floors are light wood throughout, the bedrooms upstairs have carpet. "Tem doesn't know, and she might have some design ideas."

Kade laughs. "Well, her condo is full of refreshing taste. I bet she'd do a better job than us."

"Okay, so we surprise her with an empty house and then hand over a credit card for buying shit?"

He nods emphatically. "That sounds great."

I dust off my hands and laugh. "Sold."

WE LEAD A BLINDFOLDED Saint and Artemis up the walkway. The stone is smooth under our feet. The house is lit up from within, and the glow spills out across the front. The sun has already disappeared behind the hills to our left, but the sky is brilliant shades of orange, pink, and midnight blue.

"This is ridiculous," Tem murmurs. "Can I take this off?"

"Almost." I kiss her cheek, just below the edge of the tie banded across her eyes. "It's worth it, promise."

A flutter of nerves lights up in my stomach. I *hope* it's worth it.

Beside Tem, Saint shuffles along. We stop them, and they automatically reach for each other. Their hands thread.

Saint has to know where we are. We talked to him about it, so naturally he would remember... right?

Oh God, what if we asked him and he wasn't really paying attention and he gave us a half-assed *yes* so we'd leave him alone, and he didn't realize what he was signing up for, and Kade and I just spent all this time and money and sweat building this house for us when Saint is about to have a panic attack and refuse to step foot inside it?

Kade elbows me.

"*Oof.*" I shoot him a look.

"What happened?" Tem asks. "Are you okay?"

She cranes around to peek at me, even though she can't see shit.

"All good." I glare at Kade.

The bastard just smirks at me.

"Ready?" he asks.

"So ready," Tem agrees.

He undoes the knot at the back of Saint's head, and I do the same for Tem's. I let the silk flutter away, then move around so I can see her reaction.

She blinks fast, her gaze down on the walkway. Then, slowly, it lifts to the house. She stares at it, then around. She takes in the ocean, the street at our backs...

Here it comes.

"I burned it down."

Saint scoffs. But his expression is full of wonder, too. "You did us a favor with that. This is... better."

"And that's just the outside," Kade rumbles. He gestures for the front door.

Tem leads the way. She doesn't hesitate, although she

does seem confused. Her brows remain furrowed. Saint trails after her, and Kade and I exchange a glance.

"You suddenly get nervous?" I whisper.

He nods quickly.

Great. Butterflies fully engaged, we follow them up the wide porch steps and in through the front door.

Tem spins in a slow circle in the middle of the living room, which is straight through the foyer and down a short hall. She bypassed the staircase and arched doorway to the formal dining room. The kitchen is on the left off the living room, all wide open with a huge island. For, uh, entertaining.

The chandelier our contractor hung in the living room earlier today makes her golden dress sparkle.

Tonight also happens to be the grand reopening of Bow & Arrow for Sterling Falls residents. Tourism hasn't rebounded yet, but as we ease into the warmer months, there's been a general optimism about it.

We all need a healthy dose of optimism, these days.

"This is... ours?" Tem's voice is timid and not at all like her.

"If you want to share it with us," Kade replies. He takes her hand. "What do you think?"

"I..." She focuses on Saint. "You're okay with being here?"

He nods and offers her a quick smile. "They checked before, and yeah—I'm more than okay making a life here with you."

Tears fill her eyes.

"All of you," he finishes.

Kade grins and spreads his arms. "Family."

"Family," we echo.

We already survived the worst. Now, hopefully, ahead of is only *the better*.

THE END

WHERE TO FIND SARA

Thank you so much for coming along on this crazy journey with me.

If you like my stories, I'd highly encourage you to come join my Facebook group, S. Massery Squad. There's a lot of fun stuff happening in there, and they're who I go to for polls about future books, where I share teasers, etc!

My Patreon is also an awesome place to connect and get exclusive content! On release months, I do signed paperbacks. Plus, get ARCs, audiobooks, and artwork before the rest of the world. Find me here: http://patreon.com/smassery

And last but not least, here are some social media links for ya:

Facebook: Author S Massery
Instagram: @authorsmassery
Tiktok: @smassery
Goodreads: S. Massery
Bookbub: S. Massery

ALSO BY S. MASSERY

Hockey Gods

Brutal Obsession

Devious Obsession

Secret Obsession

Twisted Obsession

Fierce Obsession

Hockey Titans

Into Ruin

Ruined God

Shadow Valley U

Sticks & Stones

Heart of Thorns

SVU 3

The Christmas Playbook

Standalone Hockey

The Pucking Coach's Daughter

Fallen Royals

Wicked Dreams

Wicked Games

Wicked Promises

Cruel Abandon

Vicious Desire

Wild Fury

Sterling Falls

#0 Thrill

#1 Thief

#2 Fighter

#3 Rebel

#4 Queen

Sterling Falls Rogues

#0 Terror

#1 Nemesis

#2 Warrior

#3 Martyr

#4 Saint

DeSantis Mafia

#1 Ruthless Saint

#2 Savage Prince

#3 Stolen Crown

Broken Mercenaries

#1 Blood Sky

#2 Angel of Death

#3 Morning Star

More at http://smassery.com

ABOUT THE AUTHOR

S. Massery is a dark romance author who loves injecting a good dose of suspense into her stories. Originally from Massachusetts, she now lives in Southern California with her dog, Alice.

Before adventuring into the world of writing, she went to college in Boston and held a wide variety of jobs—including working on a dude ranch in Wyoming (a personal highlight). She has a love affair with coffee and chocolate. When S. Massery isn't writing, she can be found devouring books, playing outside with her dog, or trying to make people smile.

www.ingramcontent.com/pod-product-compliance
Lightning Source LLC
Chambersburg PA
CBHW061640190726
48289CB00006B/1677